I0571373

Until The Water Bleeds

Ray Stern

Copyright © 2025 by Ray Stern

All rights reserved.

No portion of this book may be reproduced in any form without written permission from the publisher or author, except as permitted by U.S. copyright law.

Visit www.ray-stern-books.com

Cover created by GetCovers.com

CONTENTS

DEDICATION

T his book is dedicated to my Dad, who passed before he could
read it.
I love you, Dad, and I hope that you are proud of me.

Prologue

Darkness. It devoured everything.

The sliver of moon above was barely bright enough to cast light through the dense canopy of trees that surrounded her.

The effort to stay quiet was becoming increasingly difficult the longer Stephanie's mind played tricks on her. Each sound, every shadow, was the monster she was running from.

What had started as a typical night with friends had turned into every woman's worst nightmare - being hunted by a stranger.

At first, there had been sneaking glances at the bar, then easy banter and flirting, and finally the decision to throw caution to the wind and leave with the person for some privacy.

Now she was running for her life in the stifling air of the woods she'd fled into.

A twig snapped to the right, and Stephanie held her breath. Crouched against a large tree, she closed her eyes and tried to slow her breathing.

"You can't hide forever," a voice called out, the elation sending shivers down Stephanie's spine. "I will catch you."

She clasped a hand over her mouth to stifle her sob as she shook her head and prayed for rescue.

She knew, God, she knew, that no one was coming.

Her friends thought she'd gone home with the stranger, cheering her on in their drunkenness.

Why did she ever think it was a good idea to go home with someone she didn't know? All she wanted was one night of worry-free fun while she was on vacation.

"Boo." The gleeful whisper came right by her ear, and Stephanie screamed. Hands seized her, hoisting her from her crouch and slammed her back into the tree.

She fought with everything in her to break free, but they were faster and stronger.

"That's cute," they chuckled, catching her wrist and pinning it above her head, breath hot against her ear. "But I win."

Searing pain exploded in her stomach, stealing the breath from her lungs. The knife slid in with terrifying ease. A scream got caught in her throat as the blade was yanked free and was then driven in again. She felt the warmth begin to pour down her stomach, the air becoming heavy with the metallic tang of blood.

The void closed in as her legs buckled, and she collapsed.

Crying, scrambling in the dirt.

Trying to cling to life.

They watched from a few feet away as Stephanie dragged herself across the forest floor, her movements becoming sluggish.

Blood soaked her shirt, her hands, and the ground beneath her. The dirt churned through her fingers as she clawed her way through the forest's leaves.

She continued to put one hand in front of the other, but her body faltered, no longer under her command.

She pictured her friends, her family, her life.

It wouldn't take long now for the wounds inflicted to rob her of the life she had left.

Stephanie stopped fighting, realizing her fate. Her beloved cat back home would wonder where she was. She would never fulfill the dreams she had for her future: meeting someone, starting a family, and growing old.

Their face blurred as her vision swam.

"Why?" she whispered.

They approached, their shoes crunching on the dry leaves, and smiled.

They bent down to lean in closer. "Why not?"

They caressed her face with chilling gentleness.

The last thing she saw was their eyes, bright with twisted excitement.

Chapter One

"Fuck." My breath hitches as a warm, wet tongue drags a slow line up my neck.

Bright lights flash, shifting in sync with the heavy EDM beat pounding throughout the club. Pulsing with color, they give club-goers as much, or as little, privacy as they want. Shadows along the outskirts of the dance floor cast enough darkness for those wishing to hide in the nooks along the walls, while the center of the dance floor is illuminated for those preferring to see and be seen by others.

I'm currently in one of those dark corners, shoved against the wall by my ex-girlfriend Danielle after one too many tequila shots.

Tightening my grip in her tangled hair, I pull a low moan from her.

Suddenly, the tongue on my neck is gone, and I can't help but let out a whimper at its loss before it's quickly replaced by teeth nipping at the sensitive skin. My head falls back against the wall as her mouth trails lower.

Familiar perfume floods my senses, and I barely register her hand slipping beneath the hem of my shirt until warm fingers splay across my stomach.

"Jesus Christ." I groan and crash my lips back to hers, shoving off the wall and spinning us around.

Now she's pinned, my thigh slotted between her legs.

"Lex." Danielle gasps, grinding down.

Smiling into the kiss, I move my hands to her belt, uncaring that we can be caught at any moment.

I'm about to slide my hand lower when a firm grip clamps down on my shoulder, jerking me back to reality.

"Well, well. I should've known that you'd be here being a slut, Danielle." A familiar voice drawls disdainfully behind me before I feel a hand on my waist and I'm dragged backwards into the body of Riley, my best friend.

She then steps between us, towering over Danielle. "Don't you have a boyfriend to run back to?" She seethes.

Danielle drags her thumb across her lower lip. "Riley." She sneers as she buckles her belt. "Good to see you, as always. Is it a coincidence that you always seem to come between us?"

Rolling my eyes at the two, I speak before Riley can. "Alrighty. This has been great. I'll see you later, Dani."

They've never gotten along, and their dislike for each other only got stronger the longer Danielle and I were together.

"Are you serious?" Danielle scoffs behind us. "Fuck you, Whitlock." She yells at our backs.

"Not tonight!" Riley calls out over her shoulder, her voice singsong, and her middle finger high in the air. She loops her arm in mine and turns her attention to me once we have walked a short distance away.

"What the fuck, Lexi?" She husks in my ear, her breath tickling my neck, as we weave through clubgoers to the outside balcony.

"I'm just having a little fun." I shrug. "It's not a big deal."

"It is." Her voice is solemn.

The lighting is more consistent when we reach the patio, the music thudding dully behind us. Our group is gathered around a table, drinks in hand, laughing. The March weather is perfect, and I can't deny that it's a pleasant reprieve from the sweltering dance floor.

Riley drops into the only empty chair and gestures grandly. "Guess where I found this one?"

Elbowing her, I throw my arm around her shoulders and lean on her. "Why is everyone sitting instead of dancing?"

Andrea, my older sister, who acts like our mother half the time, squints her eyes at me and then glares.

"Why do you have lipstick all over your face?" Her eyes go wide. "Alexandria Whitlock, please tell me you did not."

I open my mouth to answer, but Riley beats me to it. "She did." She nods gravely.

Andrea shakes her head at me. "Lexi, I love you, but you have got to stay away from Dani."

"You suck." I poke Riley before turning to my overprotective older sister. "It's fine. Riley saved me from the big, bad ex-girlfriend. Let's move on." I wave my hand in the air. "Again, I ask, why are we not dancing?"

Around the table, the five others watch on in amusement. We've been friends since high school, the eight of us, even though we spanned a few grades. George and Hannah were in the same grade as me and Riley, while Pru and Claire were two grades above us with Andrea and Sean. Everyone is coupled up except me and Riley, who have been best friends since freshman year of high school.

"Hannah got too hot, so we took a break," George explains, his arm loosely thrown around the back of her chair.

"Then we got comfortable and just haven't moved," Claire adds.

"We're planning Dre's graduation trip. How do we feel about New York?" Sean smiles his crooked grin and squeezes the hand on Andrea's thigh.

"We've already been a couple of times before," I answer. "Why don't we find a new place to go? Graduating with your Master's deserves something big." Reaching across the table, I try to grab Andrea's drink, but she slaps my hand away.

"What about Hawaii?" George suggests, sliding his beer toward me. "Here. I'm done."

Hannah sips a drink next to him, bobbing her head to the beat of the music filtering onto the patio.

I sip the offered drink and tip it in thanks. "Hawaii could be fun. We haven't been there." I look at Andrea. "You've always wanted to learn how to surf."

"I have family in Hawaii," Pru says, her head leaning on Claire's shoulder. "I'm sure we can stay with them."

Claire watches with a relaxed smile as she runs her fingers through Pru's short hair. "I just got back from a business trip there. It was gorgeous. I wouldn't say no to going back."

Andrea perks up. "That's a good idea!"

"Wait. No. I'm terrified of the ocean." Sean says in alarm. "It's too big. There are too many things you can't see in the ocean."

My focus shifts away from the group as I catch Danielle walking onto the patio from the corner of my eye. She doesn't glance our way as she strides toward a tall guy and pulls him into a heated kiss. My brow raises, and I have to choke down a gag. When she finally breaks the kiss and makes direct eye contact with me, she smirks before turning away again.

"Ignore her," Riley whispers in my ear, her jaw clenched. "Let him have her."

"Oh, I'm not worried about her." Turning to face Riley, I nudge her.

It's the truth. Everyone thinks Danielle broke up with me, but I'm the one who kicked her ass to the curb. I know she's trying to make me jealous, but she doesn't realize I don't care.

Riley squeaks as I pull her from her chair. "I want to dance." I down the rest of my beer and slam the glass on the table. "We are in the middle of a club. Let's dance now and discuss this over brunch tomorrow."

Andrea shrugs and finishes her drink as well. "You heard the woman. Let's dance!"

***

The following day, I groan as sunlight slips through a crack in the blinds, hitting me right in the eyes. My head throbs instantly, an unwelcome reminder of every drink I had the night before.

I shift and turn to face the other way to escape the light, but instead of finding cool sheets, I roll right into a warm body beside me. My heart skips a beat, my hangover momentarily forgotten as I panic. I bolt upright, scrambling away from the person and almost falling off the edge of the bed in the process. Clothes are strewn across the floor, there's a brunette in my bed, and I hurriedly look to make sure I'm wearing clothes.

"Either go back to bed or make me some coffee," Riley mumbles, swatting her hand out to smack at me.

Heaving a sigh of relief, I relax, lying back down and holding my head that is currently pounding from the sudden movement. "Thank fuck."

She pokes her head up to look at me and raises an eyebrow. "Were you expecting someone else?" The sarcasm in her voice is thick.

"For a second, I was worried that I was an idiot and had taken Dani home. Thank God it's you."

Riley rolls her eyes as she shoves her head back into her pillow. "Someone has to make sure you don't regret your entire life in the morning." Her voice is muffled. "I was serious about the coffee. Get on it." She blindly waves an arm out to shoo me away.

Playfully smacking her ass, I peel back the covers and slowly get out of bed. "Why do I have to make the coffee?" I grumble as I stretch my arms over my head.

She opens one eye to stare at me. "If I have to get out of this bed to make the coffee, I will murder you. That's why." Her eye dips down to the sliver of skin exposed between my shirt and shorts before snapping back to mine.

I try not to notice, but my cheeks heat up anyway.

Jesus.

I slide my feet into my slippers and pad my way to the bathroom.

I stare at myself in the mirror as I wash my hands and wince at my reflection. My shoulder-length blonde hair is half sticking up in places, and my usually blue eyes are dull with dark circles beneath them.

Don't I look like a treat...

Yawning as I reach the kitchen, I blindly reach into a cabinet to grab the coffee bag. As I prep the coffee maker, I try to piece together what happened last night after we went back inside to dance. There were more shots, there was more dancing, and then there was nothing.

What a fucking shit show.

I lean on the counter, waiting for the coffee to brew, and put my head in my hands.

"Yeah, my thoughts exactly." Riley breezes through the kitchen and shoves past me to get to the fridge. "Have fun last night?" She goads.

I stand up and smile appreciatively. "You're a good friend," I say softly.

Riley looks at me for a long moment and then shrugs. "Someone has to keep you in check."

I stare at her and take in the long legs on display under the T-shirt she slept in, her brown hair mussed and her green eyes bright, and my heart beats faster against my will.

"What time are we meeting everyone?" I ask through another yawn.

"11. I would say it's probably in your best interest to shower before we go." Riley crinkles her nose. "You, my dear, smell like a distillery." She waves a hand in front of her nose.

My brow arches. "You know, you're not smelling so hot yourself, Conner."

"After everything I've done for you?" She clutches her chest in mock betrayal. "You wound me."

CHAPTER TWO

I glance at my watch and groan as we approach the restaurant. We're 15 minutes late to meet everyone, thanks to Riley taking her sweet ass time getting ready. I mentally prepare myself for the ribbing we're about to get.

"Well, well, well," Andrea teases as we join everyone at the table. "Look what the cat dragged in." She gives me an evil smile. "You both look great!" She yells in my ear.

At least that's what it feels like with the shrill tone of her voice so early in the morning.

Wincing, I sink into an empty chair next to Hannah. "Dre, don't even start with me." I point a warning finger at her as Hannah pats my back.

"I would kill someone for a mimosa and avocado toast right now." Riley sighs dramatically and sits, not taking off her sunglasses even though we're inside.

"You're in a violent mood today," I tell her. "She threatened to murder me over coffee earlier," I explain to the rest of the table.

Riley waves me off and starts a conversation with Pru about the healing power of mimosas.

"So, vacation," George says, sipping his Bloody Mary and looking expectantly at the rest of the table.

"We literally don't even have our food yet," Pru grumbles, apparently just as moody as Riley this morning.

We fall into easy conversation as menus are passed and drink orders go in. Most of them are alcoholic, with Riley mumbling something about "hair of the dog" or whatever.

It's been a while since we've all had a weekend together, with how hectic our lives have been. Sean and Claire are catching up on work, both being in the financial field, while Hannah and Andrea are talking about the current books they are reading. I sit back and observe, enjoying the easy banter and conversation that flows between everyone.

We get our food and immediately dig in, and I have to prevent myself from stabbing Riley with my fork when she goes for a bite of my pancakes.

Pru sets her fork down after a few bites of her omelet, looking a little less angry than she previously did. "Okay, I'm ready to talk about vacation."

"Oh, good. I'm so glad you're ready now," Claire teases, nudging Pru gently.

Pru ignores her. "Hawaii? Good or bad idea?"

George nods, his smile lighting up his face. "I think it's great." He has to speak around a mouthful of Eggs Benedict.

"Can we do something not surrounded by the ocean?" Sean asks. "Has no one seen Sharknado? What if we get stuck in the middle of a storm?"

"We're not going to-"

"What about a cruise?" Riley pipes up from around the rim of her second mimosa, interrupting Andrea.

Sean groans and slouches in his chair. "A cruise is even worse!"

Andrea's eyes light up. She slams her hand on the table excitedly, then points at Riley. "Yes! We could all use a good break from the real world."

Riley's smile is smug. "My thoughts exactly."

Chuckling, I sip my own Bloody Mary. "Don't we need to plan pretty far out for a cruise?   Not to be a Debbie Downer, but that sounds like it won't be anytime soon."

"Actually, you can find some really good deals on cruises. They have them all year long," Claire says. "I get emails all the time after Pru and I went the other year."

George puts another bite of food in his mouth and chews, a contemplative look on his face. He swallows and sets his fork down. "I could do a cruise." He nods.

Hannah smiles and bounces in her seat a little. "I've never been on a cruise but always wanted to."

"Sharks, people," Sean says.

"Sean, there are no sharks on a cruise ship," Riley laughs, exasperated.

"Storms!" He yells and winces in embarrassment as the table beside us looks our way.

"You need to drink some more." Pru raises an eyebrow as Claire waves at the people staring.

Sean obeys and chugs his drink, signaling our server for another.

I reach across Hannah and pat his arm. "Chances of a shark-filled storm are, I'm guessing, slim to none, bud."

"I want to swim with the sharks!" Andrea teases, and Sean goes white as a ghost.

***

After brunch, we all head back to my place to search for cruises and look at airfare. I lucked out on a sweet deal renting a room where my landlord travels 90 percent of the time, and I usually have the place to myself. All I have to do is make sure things are kept up and the house doesn't burn down.

Sean and George set themselves up on my Xbox and have been yelling at the TV ever since, while the rest of us lounge on the couches, shopping for cruises and flights.

"Why are you looking at Miami?" Hannah wonders, peering over Riley's shoulder. "I've heard that is the worst for trying to cruise out of."

"Where do you propose we sail out of then?" Riley huffs, her fingers hovering over her keyboard.

"What about L.A.?" George asks as he smashes buttons on the controller.

Hannah shoots a glare in his direction. "That's even worse."

Riley hands Hannah the laptop and stands, going to the kitchen and opening the fridge. She pulls out a beer and chugs half of it.

Okay, so I might not have a full-time roommate, but Riley is here enough that we should probably just get a place together.

"Why do we have to live in Colorado instead of at the beach?" Andrea sighs wistfully.

"Because we have mountains," Claire says. "And I would take the mountains over the beach any day."

"Wait," Pru turns to her girlfriend. "I thought you said we could move to a beach someday."

"Someday. Not this day." She kisses Pru on the cheek. "Look at cruises out of New Orleans or Galveston. The ports looked better on the cruises sailing from there."

"You son of a bitch!" Sean yells, sighing heavily as he sets his controller down and crosses his arms. "I almost had you."

"I don't know why you try to beat me. It never works for you," George says arrogantly.

"Does this mean that you two are going to help us make decisions now?" Pru asks.

Sean raises an eyebrow. "We were listening."

"Listening and helping are two very different things," Andrea ruffles his hair. "Put away the game and help us."

Hannah looks up from Riley's laptop and appraises the group. "Galveston or New Orleans?"

"Is that even a question?" Riley wonders.

"Galveston, obviously," Claire bites back a smile.

"Get out." I point at the door and glare at Claire from my spot on the couch.

Pru wraps her arm protectively around the woman. "If she goes, I go."

I wave. "Buh-bye then!" I give them my most cheerful smile.

Pru rolls her eyes and smacks my leg. Riley comes over with another beer, lifts my legs, sits down, and rests my legs over hers. I sit up and reach for her beer, causing her to pout.

"Look, we can leave out of New Orleans, but this is not about to turn into some Spring Break, Riley flashes her tits everywhere kind of trip," Andrea says.

Riley's mouth drops open, and I can't help but guffaw, the others joining in.

"I'd be offended, but last time I had a couple of Hurricanes on Bourbon Street, that's exactly what happened." Riley grins.

"I know," Andrea grimaces. "I was there and saw way more of you than I ever needed to."

"It wasn't even Mardi Gras." Claire laughs.

"So, back to the cruise planning!" Sean claps his hands and avoids looking at Riley.

Sean and Andrea have been together long enough that, as much as I view Sean as a big brother, they both view Riley as another little sister since we've been best friends for so long.

"Where is the cheapest place to fly into? And which terminal is the closest to the airport?" George asks.

I raise a brow and stare at him. "Those are actually good questions."

George does a little bow in his seat.

Hannah types on Riley's laptop while we all stare at the ceiling. Hannah is a control freak, almost worse than Andrea, and it won't matter what anyone else says unless she sees it for herself.

"New Orleans it is," she announces and sits back with a relieved sigh.

Riley opens her mouth to say something, but I put my hand over it to silence her. "No Bourbon Street!"

CHAPTER THREE

Two months later, Andrea graduates. Only days after, we find ourselves at the airport, half-asleep, over-caffeinated, and ready to board
an early flight to New Orleans.

Standing in line, Hannah leans on George and yawns every few
moments. Sean and Andrea look at something on Andrea's phone,
and Pru and Claire stand patiently while we wait to board.

Riley looks at my ticket again. "Why do you get the window seat?"

"Because I hate flying," I explain for the eightieth time.

Hannah yawns again. "Rye, you can have my window seat."

Riley stares at the redhead. "But then I can't sit next to Lex."

"You are impossible." Pru points out.

Riley scowls at Pru, who only laughs.

"I still think this is a terrible idea." Sean looks around, wringing his
hands. "I have a really bad feeling about this."

George moves towards the other man, making Hannah stumble to
catch her balance at the sudden shift, and he puts him in a headlock.

"I'll give you something to feel bad about," he jokes as Sean squawks.

Andrea sighs. "We haven't even left yet, and none of you can behave."

Claire and Hannah protest, and Andrea closes her eyes and shakes her head.

***

After we land, it's a race to baggage claim and then to the shuttle. Thankfully, there are no hiccups from the airport to the cruise terminal. We check in, drop off our bags, and drag ourselves to the main deck while we wait to embark for our first stop - Mexico.

"Ah, sunlight and good-looking half-naked..." An incredibly hairy man in a Speedo walks past us, and Riley abruptly stops talking, pushing her sunglasses back up her nose. "Yep, it's time for a drink."

I laugh and shrug my backpack up my arm. "We just stepped on the ship, Rye. Can't you wait five minutes?"

Riley shakes her head vigorously. "Absolutely not."

"I could use a drink," Sean chimes in.

I notice he is gripping Andrea's hand so hard that my poor sister is wincing. He's looking over his shoulder toward the gangway, and I can see that his eyes are glazed over.

Andrea gently pries her hand away and rubs it. "Babe, we haven't even left the terminal. Look," she points his face toward where there are still land and buildings, "you can't even see the ocean yet." She pats his cheek.

Pru spots an open table on the deck, grabs Claire, and bolts for it. "I'll take a rum and Coke!" She calls over her shoulder as she almost bowls over a small child running in and out of people on the deck. Pru glares at his parents as they stand together, oblivious to what their child is doing.

Hannah chuckles. "This trip is going to be a shit show, isn't it?" She pushes her hair behind her ear, a nervous tic of hers.

Andrea whirls around to face her. "It absolutely will not be. We are going to have a great time." She says, teeth grit and eyes glaring daggers at us.

I search around and then twirl toward the bar, laughing as I grab Riley's elbow to drag her along. "Face it, Dre, we're stuck on a giant boat with nothing to do but get hammered."

"Alexandria Whitlock, I swear to God... I'm blaming you forever if anything goes wrong this trip." Andrea stomps her foot in a full-on hissy fit.

I just wave at her and line up with Riley at the nearest bar.

"What does she think we're supposed to do on a cruise? I thought the whole point was to get wasted and not worry about real life," I say.

"She probably expects us to play Bingo, dress up for dinner, and act classy," she wiggles her eyebrows.

"I plan on doing all of the above... drunk off my ass." I smile and begin to people-watch.

The Lido Deck is getting packed. People are juggling drinks, carrying trays of food, and stray kids are everywhere.

Thanks to early check-in, we're stuck with our carry-ons until our cabins are ready. Riley, being Riley, only has her purse, the bikini she chose for the day nicely tucked inside. She told me earlier she wouldn't need anything, but I knew better than to trust that. I left room in my backpack for her clothes and packed essentials, such as sunscreen, that she had forgotten.

We stand in comfortable silence, waiting for our turn. The sun is shining, and I can already smell the sunscreen and pina colada. I can't wait to forget about everything for a little while and have fun with everyone without interruptions.

I look toward the rest of our group and observe Andrea fawning over Sean, who is looking increasingly greener by the second. Pru and Claire are snuggled up next to each other while   Pru glares at the rogue child she almost ran over. George and Hannah are off to the side, talking to each other in hushed tones and looking around as Hannah gestures with her hands.

I break the silence with a chuckle. "This is definitely going to be an interesting trip." I lean in with a wicked smile. "Who do we think is going to have a meltdown first? Sean or Hannah?"

We watch Sean nod his head in defeat at whatever Andrea is telling him, and Hannah storms off from George toward one of the dining areas, jumping as someone steps in front of her.

Riley hides a smile behind her hand. "I bet you $10 it'll be Andrea." She looks at my sister, who does seem stressed out to the max.

I scoff. "No way. She'll mellow out after a few drinks. My bet's on Hannah. She's been acting... off lately."

It's true. Hannah has always been more tightly wound than the others in the group, but lately her mood has been all over the place, and she's been more withdrawn than usual. She and George don't typically have tiffs in front of us like they just did.

Riley sticks out her hand. "Deal."

I shake the hand outstretched in front of me with a laugh as we finally make our way to the front of the line. Before I can even open my mouth to order, a man already in his swim trunks who appears to be in his early 30s cuts in front of us and starts barking out numerous drink orders.

"Yo, man, not cool," I grumble, earning an apologetic look from the bartender.

"Hey there." The guy says, turning his attention to us and smirking at Riley. He doesn't bother to hide his predatory glance up and down her body.

My fists clench at my side.

Riley squares her shoulders and raises a brow. "Not if you were the last person on earth, jackass." Faux sweetness dripping off every word.

"I'll be seeing you." He smirks as he grabs his drinks and walks off to a group of men who look to be the same age. They're all shirtless and acting like a bunch of unsupervised teenagers.

"What an overgrown frat-tastic douche." Riley scowls.

I turn to watch the men stare at us, laughing and shoving each other as they whistle in our direction. One guy, younger than the rest, isn't a part of their antics. He gives me an apologetic look and a shrug as we make eye contact.

I stare back, offering nothing in return.

Turning to the bartender, I summon my sweetest smile. "I will give you twenty bucks to make their next round weak as shit."

She throws her head back and laughs. "Ten and it's done. Starting the cruise off with a fruity cocktail?" She asks, her eyes flittering down my body before locking on mine.

I notice Riley tense out of the corner of my eye, but I blink, and she is relaxed again.

I smirk. "Absolutely not. I'll take a margarita, please. On the rocks."

Riley scoots closer to me and cuts in before the woman can respond. "I'd like a bucket of beer, a rum and Coke, and a Long Island, if that's okay with you."

The bartender looks between us and raises a brow before turning around, grabbing a bucket and some beer bottles.

I touch Rylie's arm. "You good?" I squeeze gently.

She doesn't make eye contact, and her smile doesn't reach her eyes, but she chirps out a "Never better!" Then she frowns. "I was going to change into my suit, but with those assholes over there, I think I'd better wait."

I glance at the group of men again, but they have moved on to another target—a group of women already in their bikinis.

"Probably for the best." I agree, watching her for a beat longer before grabbing our drinks and heading to the table.

"I don't understand how parents can let their kids roam free." Pru is complaining as we pass out the drinks and sit down. "Like, there are a million strangers on this boat, and this crotch goblin is just free as a bird."

Claire smiles at me as I pass her drink to her. "Babe, being a parent isn't easy. You should think about how terrible you were as a kid." She leans over to place a short kiss on Pru's lips.

God, they are disgustingly cute.

I look at Pru with her short hair and heavy eyeliner and Claire with her long hair and no makeup, and I think about how perfectly opposite they are. Somehow, it works. It really works. I watch them and their easy banter, and my heart squeezes.

It must be the tequila giving me heartburn.

With a defeated look, Pru grumbles under her breath but throws her arm over the back of Claire's chair. "Thanks for getting the drinks, guys." She says to me and Riley.

George and Hannah join us with plates of food. Riley passes them their beers and steals a fry off Hannah's plate, stating she had to pay the fry tax to sit at the table.

"You can go get your own." Hannah whacks at Riley's hand as she goes for another. "The buffet is open."

Riley makes a face. "I already stood in line for drinks. I don't want to wait in another line."

George holds up his phone and wiggles it in the air. "Did everyone download the app so we can message each other once we get going? We won't have cell service, so we need to make sure we can still talk when we're not together."

"What do you mean 'when we're not together'? I'm going to be with one of you at all times," Sean chugs his beer. "Do not leave me on this floating death trap alone."

"Oh my God. You are going to be fine. Sharknado can't hurt you." I tease.

Hannah hands Sean her beer and smiles at him as he drinks that too.

"Excuse me." A confident voice says from behind me. I turn to face the man, but he is looking at Riley. It's the younger guy from earlier, the one who looked embarrassed by his douche bag friend's behavior. "Just wanted to swing by and apologize for my friend earlier. He doesn't get out much." He smiles, playing with a bracelet on his wrist.

Everyone at the table stops talking and looks at him. I observe that he doesn't look at anyone but Riley, who sits up a little straighter in her chair. "They probably shouldn't be off-leash until they are properly trained, " she says with an arched brow.

The man chuckles. "Don't I know it." He gives her a smirk.

"Seems like you're no better at the moment," I mutter, and Riley kicks me under the table.

The man finally acknowledges the rest of the group with a nod. "Anyway, I'll leave you be. I just saw you sitting over here and wanted to swing by. I'm James, by the way."

"Thanks, James." I bite out. "Have a good cruise." I give him a tense smile.

James's eyes focus back on Rye and dip a bit too low to be only friendly before he offers a slow, knowing smile in her direction. "I hope I run into you again."

I narrow my eyes, but she smiles. "We'll see." She tilts her head, and I bite my tongue and take another sip of my margarita.

Leave it to my best friend to have people falling all over her before we've even checked into our cabins. I mean, I get it. She's stunning, with those green eyes and that long, wavy hair, but Jesus. I know it's not her fault; she's basically temptation on legs, but sometimes my heart does this stupid flip when Riley flirts with someone.

James nods before he turns and walks away. Everyone turns to stare at Riley, who is oblivious and drinking her Long Island.

"Dude..." Claire laughs. "We haven't even been on this ship for an hour, and already people are falling at your feet."

Riley scrunches her nose. "I have no idea what you're talking about. Besides, the bartender was flirting with Lexi first."

Like it's a competition I wasn't aware of or something.

I guess that happens when we both garner attention wherever we go together.

"So, what's the plan?" Andrea derails the conversation. "Does anyone see anything interesting that they want to do today?"

"There is trivia in about 30 minutes in the atrium, " George says, looking at his watch.

"What time can we get into our cabins?" Hannah counters. "A nap sounds great right about now," she punctuates with a yawn.

Pru looks at Hannah, aghast. "Ma'am, we are on a giant ass cruise ship. You can sleep later tonight. Right now is for drinking and having fun."

Sean yawns as well. "You know, a nap doesn't sound terrible."

Andrea stands up and places a hand on Sean's shoulder. "Trivia. With our powers combined..." she trails off with a devious grin.

***

Surprisingly, we found a table in the Atrium with almost enough room for all of us. Andrea, Hannah, Sean, Claire, and I are all sitting down, with Riley, George, and Pru standing behind us, squeezed in close. The overly peppy crew member in charge of trivia is standing in front, spewing all the rules.

We, of course, are arguing over a team name and not paying attention.

"We are not naming ourselves *Ship Happens*," Riley looks at me in exasperation. "What's wrong with *Tropic like it's Hot*?" She demands.

"No way in hell." Sean shakes his head.

Pru shrugs. "I like it."

"*Hot Mess Express*," Andrea announces suddenly and types into the iPad. While we were arguing, she apparently took it upon herself to answer. "You also probably missed where they announced that today's prize is drink vouchers. So, all of you bring your A-game and focus."

"Okay, teams!" The crew member claps his hands. "First question is..."

All of a sudden, I feel like someone is watching us. I look around and notice James and his group of douchebags at a table across the room, and he is staring in our direction.

Staring at Riley, to be specific.

He catches my eye, and I narrow mine at him. He blinks and looks away.

I will kick this man's ass if I have to.

A hand lands on my shoulder, and brown hair appears in my vision as Riley leans down.

"You just got super tense. Are you okay?" she murmurs, her breath hot against my ear. I catch a whiff of the Long Islands she's been drinking all day.

"I'm good." I turn my head to answer.

I don't realize how close her face is to mine.

My eyes immediately go to her lips before I force them back up.

I can see the light dusting of freckles on her nose this close.

I hear her breath hitch.

I freeze.

Then my brain kicks in, and I realize our proximity and how easy it would be to lean in, and I quickly face forward again.

Acting like I didn't almost kiss my best friend.

"Yo, lesbians," Pru calls out with a snap of her fingers in our direction. "Are you going to help answer questions or just be drunk idiots all day?"

"I'm not a lesbian. I'm bi," Riley corrects. "There's a difference."

Claire snorts. "Yeah, you still haven't realized that penis isn't that great."

"Okay!" Sean claps his hands. "Can we do this later and focus on trivia now?"

The screen shows another question: *What year did the Titanic sink?*

"Oh, come on!" Sean groans, and we all laugh hysterically.

CHAPTER FOUR

After losing trivia, to absolutely no one's surprise, our cabins were finally ready. We all split off to unpack and unwind before dinner; Riley went to shower, the rest went to their cabins, and I went to drink with Andrea. We had all decided to forgo the Sail-Away party to relax after a long day of traveling.

After Dre and I finished our drinks, we promised to meet in forty-five minutes.

Now, walking the ship's halls, I pass decorated cabin doors and groups of laughing strangers, and I can't help but feel weirdly giddy.

Maybe it's the ocean air. Or maybe it's the anticipation.

I unlock the door to our cabin and call out, "Honey, I'm home!"

I walk inside and stop dead in my tracks when I see Riley.

Standing at the mirror applying her lipstick, her eyes meet mine through the glass, and she winks. "Took you long enough. I'm hungry. Get dressed."

Riley's wearing a red dress that hits mid-thigh and shows just enough cleavage to melt my brain. It's like the dress was designed specifically to fuck with me.

I stare, open-mouthed, before I even realize what I'm doing.

She gives me a look like I've grown a second head.

"You look beautiful." The words leave my mouth, huskier than usual, before my brain can even protest.

Riley's cheeks flush pink, and I clear my throat.

"Let me get changed. Then we can meet up with everyone and eat." I force myself to move further into the room.

"Perfect." Riley smiles, her eyes sparkling as she passes me to get to the bathroom. Her fingers brush mine, making them tingle, and my heart skips.

This isn't just a crush. It hasn't been for a long time.

Before I spiral entirely, I shake my head to snap myself out of it.

"Clothes," I tell myself, and go to the small closet and open the doors.

Get it together, Whitlock.

***

Forty-five minutes later, as promised, we head to the Main Dining Room. Riley and I walk in comfortable silence as we navigate the crowd. There's quite the mix: those dressed up for dinner, others still in swimsuits, and some wandering aimlessly.

The cool evening air swirls in from the constant opening and closing of the doors, and it feels like we are on a completely different planet.

Reaching the lobby outside the dining room, we find our group and head over. Riley, Andrea, Hannah, and Claire are all in dresses, while the rest wear slacks and button-down shirts. We're not the fancy dinner type of group, so this cruise feels like a good excuse to try something different.

"Well, don't you both look hot?" Sean smiles at us as we approach. Andrea gives him a backhanded slap to the chest. He rubs the spot and makes a hurt face at her.

"Did anyone look at the menu for tonight?" Hannah asks, her nose in her phone.

Riley perks up and wanders over to her. "Where did you find a menu?" She peers at the phone in Hannah's hand.

George sighs. "Give me your phone, Riley." He holds out a hand. "Let me download the app before it's too late."

Riley doesn't even look up as she passes her phone over. "Ooh! Lobster bisque!"

"Did you get us on the list?" I ask Andrea as the rest of the group gathers to look at the phone.

God forbid these bozos look at the giant ass menu that is posted 10 feet away from them.

"Yep!" Andrea answers. "They said about 10 minutes." She looks at her watch. "I'm guessing that 10 minutes is in Cruise Time, because it's been about 15."

As if they knew she was talking shit, we laugh as the buzzer in her hand goes off. We all gather together and make our way into the dining room, where we are brought to a table against one of the windows. Sean immediately goes to a chair with his back to the glass so he can't see the ocean. Andrea closes her eyes and takes a deep breath with an adoring smile on her lips before taking the seat next to him.

The rest of us crowd in, and the table is big enough for us, but there is still a tight squeeze.

My thigh brushes against Riley's under the table, and I fight the instinct to pull back like I've been burned. "Sorry," I mutter.

Riley gives me a look like I have completely lost it. "Are you okay? You have been super jumpy today." She places the back of her hand on my forehead. "Are you coming down with something?"

Everyone ignores us like usual, as I attempt to smack her hand away, inadvertently smacking myself in the head.

"Good evening!" a cheerful young man greets as he approaches the table. "I am Javier, and I will be taking care of you tonight. Would you like to start with any drinks? A bottle of wine or two to share?"

"A bottle of white and red would be perfect," Claire answers before anyone else can. "Whatever your house wine is will be fine."

Javier shoots us a winning smile and nods as he leaves to retrieve the wine.

We all peruse the menu again as we wait for him to return and choose what appetizers and entrees we want.

Javier quickly returns and sets the two opened bottles of wine on the table before taking our order. Once we finish, he rushes away to his next table as we distribute the wine.

Claire lifts her wine glass and looks at Andrea. "To Andrea. Congratulations on graduating, babe. We're all proud of you."

Everyone cheers and holds their drinks up for a toast. We laugh as George accidentally spills some, and Hannah rolls her eyes.

Conversation flows—talk of graduation, summer plans, what's next. I can't do much since I work at a bar and have a hard enough time getting weekends off. Honestly, I'm still shocked they let me take off for the cruise.

Our appetizers arrived fast, which is great because I didn't realize how hungry I was until we sat down and I started smelling the food.

"So, were you going to mention that you got us a king bed instead of two twins, or were you hoping I wouldn't say anything about it?" Riley says under her breath so only I hear.

My wine glass pauses at my lips.

Riley places a hand on my thigh, and I nearly spit out the sip I managed to take. She chuckles low, a sound that hits me right in the gut, but doesn't move her hand.

Then, a scream.

High. Raw.

Piercing.

Every head in the room snaps toward the sound at once. A man slumps out of his chair across the dining room as the woman sitting with him scrambles to reach him.

"What the fuck." Pru says.

"Is he choking?" George whispers, but none of us answer.

Crew members rush to the man, laying him flat on the floor. One bends down to put their ear to his mouth and shakes their head. The others immediately start CPR, and I feel my own heart beating hard in my chest.

"Oh my God," Andrea gasps.

The woman is still screaming.

She tries again to reach for him, but one of the servers is gently blocking her to keep her back so they can work. She keeps calling his name, sobbing.

"*Daniel*!"

It feels like time has stopped.

The silence in the room is haunting.

Then a fork falls onto a plate. A baby starts to cry.

Everything starts to move again.

Medical and security staff rush in with a stretcher and hurriedly load the man onto it. The woman has stopped screaming, but she is still sobbing uncontrollably. She follows the medical staff as they rush the stretcher out of the room, a young security officer gently leading her by the arm.

We all look back at each other, stunned into silence.

Past Andrea's shoulder, the ocean stretches endlessly.

This is our first day on this cruise.

Things like this aren't supposed to happen.

The rest of dinner is somber, our excitement sobered by what had happened. We finish our meals almost silently, and barely a word is said between us.

After we finish, we decide to hit one of the clubs, which would be a good way to distract ourselves from dinner and get back into carefree vacation mode.

I'm not in the mood to party, and I doubt the others are either. I know the only reason we agreed to meet up and have fun is to attempt to regain a sense of normalcy again.

***

"So that was quite the first dinner," Riley mentions as we enter our cabin. "I hope they all aren't so..." She pauses, looking for the right word. "Fucked up."

I can't help but agree.

"I don't even know if I want to go to the club." She pouts and plops down on the bed, lying back on it.

I avert my eyes from where her dress has ridden up her thighs and take a deep breath.

"Riley..." I begin.

She props herself up on her elbows to give me her full attention. "Yeah?" It's soft, maybe hopeful.

And I panic.

"Maybe James will be at the club," I say, immediately wanting to punch myself in the face.

She balks at me. "Right." She says, unemotional, and lies back down.

I tilt my head back and close my eyes, internally groaning.

What the fuck is wrong with me?

"I'm going to check out the balcony," I grumble, irritated at myself.

"I will be right here until we are ready to go."

I step onto the balcony and take a deep breath. The crisp ocean air helps clear my head a little, and I lean over the railing to look out into the sunset. The colors are gorgeous, and I know I should feel so alive now.

All I can think about is the woman's screams.

***

Like I summoned him straight from a frat party in the seventh circle of hell, James is, in fact, at the club when we get there.

"Looks like you have a chance at a cruise boyfriend, Rye." George snickers when we all notice him.

Andrea looks at me to gauge my reaction, and I give her a half smile.

Like the good, older sister she is, she knows about my feelings for Riley. She's only brought it up once, telling me, 'Lexi, I swear to the gods that I will tell her for you if you don't pull your head out of your ass and tell her yourself.'

That was about six months ago, so I'm surprised she's held it so long.

"I'm definitely not interested," Riley says, bringing me back to the moment.

Pru and Claire start to pull away from the group. "We'll grab the drinks this time."

Hannah seems even more subdued than usual, so I approach her and hook my arm through hers. "We're going to go find somewhere to sit."

"Sit? It's a fucking dance club, Lex." Riley yells after us.

We find a table in the back of the room, which is a miracle. Once we sit, I ask gently, "What's going on?"

Hannah gives me a tight-lipped smile, watching the dance floor with a blank expression. "Nothing."

"Liar. Is it what happened earlier?" I prod.

Hannah turns to look at me, and her eyes fill with tears. "It's just all so much," she whispers.

I pull her hand into my lap and hold it comfortingly. "What is?"

She suddenly shakes her head and breaks eye contact with me, pulling her hand away. "I guess it is what happened earlier. It just really threw me off. One minute we're all having fun, and the next they're doing CPR on a man."

Everyone joins us before I respond, and Pru and Claire follow with the drinks. We sit and sip our drinks for a while, trying to relax and enjoy ourselves, and as time passes, we loosen up a little.

Andrea drags Sean onto the dance floor, and George follows suit with Hannah. Pru and Claire are making out in the corner of the booth - dear God, how much wine did they have with dinner? - and Riley and I share a look of disgust before we laugh.

"Hello." James appears out of fucking nowhere. "Would you like a drink?" He asks Riley.

Smirking, Riley holds her glass up. "Got one."

James chuckles. "Can I interest you in a dance, then?"

Claire stops sucking face with Pru long enough to shove Riley out of her chair with her foot. "Go dance." Then she's on Pru's lips again.

My blood boils as I watch Riley shrug and take James' hand as he leads her out onto the floor.

I have no right to say anything. I almost fucked my ex up against the wall of a club less than two months ago.

I might be an idiot, but I'm no hypocrite.

I watch everyone, wallowing in self-pity, for about five minutes before Pru and Claire grab me by the arms.

"Come on, Casanova. Let's dance." Pru says, and I scoff.

After about an hour of dancing, all of us trading dance partners and me having to watch Riley laugh with James half the time, the brunette comes up to me with a devious smile.

"Oh no. What's that look for?" I ask hesitantly.

"I have danced with everyone here... except for you." Riley's grin widens as she pulls me to her.

Our bodies are close, and the hip-hop beat in the background matches the pounding of my heart. Riley drapes her arms over my shoulders, locks them around my neck, and starts rolling her hips to the beat.

This woman is seriously trying to kill me.

"Having fun?" She asks innocently, eyes wide with a glimmer of mischief.

"Oh sure." I nod.

She turns around and presses her back to my front. "Are you sure? Because all day you have been tense."

I close my eyes and let the sensations run over me: the loud music, the bright lights, the smell of beer, and the sweat.

Riley's ass on me.

If she wants me to relax, she's doing a really shit job because right now I can't think of anything other than the heat pooling low in my stomach.

"It's been a day." I choke out, trying to focus on the music instead of the delicious way my best friend is grinding on me.

"It has." She agrees and rolls her hips. "But I think it's getting better by the moment." She leans her head back on my shoulder, and I can see the smirk on her face from this angle.

I involuntarily tighten my arms around her waist and move my hips in rhythm with hers. My mouth has gone dry, and my whole body tingles where our bodies mesh together.

James walks up to us, face somber, and stops in front of us. "I don't mean to interrupt here, but I know you had asked if I had heard anything about that man at dinner, and I have some news." He frowns.

Riley and I stop dancing and separate, and she looks at him expectantly. "What happened?"

"He didn't make it," James sighs heavily.

"How do you even know that?" I ask.

The first thought comes to mind and goes flying out of my mouth. My whole body goes numb. I don't know how to feel, especially as I look at Riley, who has tears in her eyes.

Riley takes a deep breath and turns to me. "James is a doctor. So are his friends."

Because that's not conveniently suspicious.

"We're headed out," Sean says, suddenly at my side. "We want to sleep before what's sure to be a long day tomorrow."

I have to tell them. They were all there and deserve to know the outcome of what happened.

"James just let us know that the man from dinner died," I announce gently.

Hannah starts crying, leaning into George, whose face falls. Sean comforts Andrea as she gasps in shock, and Pru and Claire stare at us in disbelief.

"Yeah, that's enough for one day." Andrea breathes softly.

We all silently leave the club and go to our separate cabins.

It's only the first day.

People are supposed to relax and have fun on cruises, not die in the middle of dinner.

I can't help but shake what Sean had said about having a bad feeling, but tomorrow is a new day.

Tomorrow will be a better day.

CHAPTER FIVE

I wake up dizzy and confused before remembering that we're on a cruise and this is not my bedroom at home. I can feel the ship's gentle rocking, and I stretch and yawn, feeling at peace.

Then last night slams back into me, heavy and cold.

Fuck.

We watched a man die.

"Morning," Riley says gently.

She's sitting in bed with a book in her lap, a cup of coffee in her hand, and a soft smile aimed at me.

"Morning," I croak. "Where did you find coffee?"

She grabs a second cup from the side table, passing it to me as I sit up and accept it with a grateful hum.

"I've been up for a bit," she shrugs. "Hopefully it's not too cold. You slept forever."

I glance at the clock behind her and groan. "Rye, it's only eight."

"We're meeting everyone for breakfast at ten," she says. "Want to work out with me before that?"

I sigh defeatedly. "Fine. But know that I already hate you."

I take a sip of the coffee. It's perfect.

Damn her.

***

We take quick turns in the bathroom and are soon headed out the door to the gym. Riley has already scoped out where it is, because God forbid she miss a day of working out even when we're on vacation.

We take the scenic route along the outer deck, letting the fresh ocean air wake us up as we walk. The water stretches endlessly beyond the rails, calm and peaceful in the early light.

We pass by the lounge chairs on the deck where a woman is asleep on one, a book open on her chest, and a large hat pulled over her eyes. She looks like she is passed out hard, the red towel under her draped over the lounger and touching the floor.

I stop to look closer, feeling like something is off, but Riley grabs my arm and pulls me along, and I follow without complaint.

We arrive at the gym and nod at each other as we put in our earbuds. We're not strangers to working out together, seeing as how Riley is a fitness instructor and helps keep my ass in shape—literally. We're work-out buddies by default, even if half the time I hate her for getting me out of bed at ungodly hours.

We start with stretches, and after we have warmed up, she heads to a treadmill while I settle in at the leg press. We work out in silence, listening to our music, and I reflect on what has happened on this cruise so far. I can tell that Riley is doing the same because she runs faster than usual and only does that when something bothers her.

I'm just about through with my set when James strolls into the gym. His eyes light up at the sight of Riley, and I slam the weights harder than I mean to.

Please, Lord, tell me she did not tell this man we would be here.

He goes to the treadmill beside her, drapes his towel on the handrail, and puts water in the cupholder.

Riley looks over and does a double-take. "James!"

"Good morning. Fancy meeting you here." James smirks.

Riley slows her run to a walk. "Yeah, what a surprise." She looks over at me, and her eyes widen. "Too bad we were just leaving."

James frowns. "Oh, that's a bummer. Last night you told me you would be working out in the morning, and I was hoping to catch you."

"Well," she says with that tight, polite smile she wears when trying not to be rude, "I gotta go do... cruise things now." She hops off the treadmill and quickly comes over to me.

"I'll run into you later?" James asks hopefully, chest puffed out.

"Seems to be the pattern," I mutter as Riley only nods.

We gather our things quickly and leave the gym, and James, behind.

Once we're a little distance away, Riley stops. "That was... awkward, right?"

I stop too and lean against the wall. "Depends on whether you invited him or not." I shrug, trying to be nonchalant.

She shakes her head quickly. "No way. I *mentioned* I'd be working out in the morning while we chatted last night. I never said, 'Hey, come crash my cardio session and make things weird.'"

I study her and nod. "I mean..." I trail off. "It's a little stalker-like."

She shudders. "Right?"

We begin our trek back to our room to prepare for brunch with the group, but I slow down as we pass the lounge chairs from earlier.

Now, three security officers are standing around the chairs, specifically the one with the woman who had the book earlier.

Riley notices at the same time. "Yikes. Someone got a little too schwasted last night," she mumbles, miming drinking.

But I look closer, and the woman from earlier isn't moving.

"Yeah... she must really be out of it," I chuckle humorlessly, my gut twisting uncomfortably.

Riley glances again, eyebrows drawing together.

We watch security pry the book from her hand and then carefully roll her over.

Then, I realize her towel isn't supposed to be red.

It's blood.

What the fuck?

"Riley..." I whisper, and notice that she has gone completely pale next to me.

"I see it," she whispers back and starts inching slowly away, and I follow as we head back inside the ship.

Back in the room, we stop just inside the door and glance at each other, neither knowing what to say.

I bite the bullet and try to keep it light by smiling. "Rock, paper, scissors for the bathroom?"

Riley's eyes are thankful as she smirks and peels off her sweaty tank top, leaving her in a sports bra and shorts. "You could always join me," she says.

I choke on my own spit.

***

"I want like, a plate of bacon," Hannah tells our server at brunch. "Just pile that shit on there."

The server raises an eyebrow but writes down the order anyway.

Riley and I talked about what we had seen, and after much convincing on my part, we decided not to tell everyone about what had happened. I didn't want to bring everyone down again after what happened last night.

"Ooh, I'll take the French Toast!" Riley announces, face lighting up. She turns to me and winks, "We worked out hard enough this morning to warrant French Toast, don't you think?"

Andrea snorts into her orange juice, and I shoot her a warning look. Everyone else giggles, and I want to die.

Riley and I have always been flirty and bantered back and forth, but this week has been on a whole new level. I don't know if it's because I'm more aware of it right now or if Riley has stepped up her game.

I've got to stop reading into this and get my shit under control, but she's definitely making it complicated.

"What is our plan for the day?" Claire asks as she eats a cherry out of her drink. "Anyone see anything interesting on the agenda?"

"There's towel animal folding later that I want to check out." Pru slurps her mimosa.

"For someone who doesn't like kids, you sure picked an activity full of them," George laughs.

I chuckle and grab for Riley's mimosa since mine is already empty. "You don't like children because you are one, Pru."

Pru looks affronted, but Claire nods her head in agreement.

"What else is going on today?" Sean asks, pulling out his phone. "Oh! Some cool things are happening on the Lido Deck later."

I gasp. "Sean Hancock. Are you *actually* having fun?"

He lifts his margarita. "I've been drinking since I woke up. These drink packages aren't going to drink themselves."

"He'll be passed out by lunch," Andrea sighs heavily.

"Rye, you should join the sexiest legs contest." Claire slaps Riley's arm excitedly as she looks at her phone.

Riley scrunches her nose. "No, thank you. I've had enough unwanted attention for the day."

Hannah raises a brow. "Lexi bothering you that much?" She jokes, and I give her an unamused look.

"Our workout got crashed by tall, dark, and stalkery earlier," I explain.

"I'm guessing that means James?" Andrea makes a face.

"Okay, so towel animal folding, party on the Lido Deck for a while, and then dinner again? Tonight is an elegant night, and we can all get some pictures." George suggests.

We all agreed and kept the drinks flowing as we finished brunch.

***

"Rye, it's your boyfriend in the Speedo!" I laugh in drunken hysterics as we watch the hairy chest contest from the chairs we were able to snag on the Lido Deck.

She makes a fake vomiting noise and reaches out to smack me. "Disgusting, Whitlock."

Riley, Andrea, Sean, and I are all watching the contests on the deck while the other four decided to go to the adults-only area and hang out where it is a little more peaceful.

The swan I made earlier sits on the edge of my chair, and Riley keeps laughing at it. I didn't think I would have as much fun as I did, but I enjoyed myself more than anyone else.

We laugh and continue to drink, but it suddenly gets colder as I overhear the people next to us talking.

"Yeah, there were like 10 security officers around her. Peggy asked one of them what happened, and they told her there had been an 'accident' and the area would be closed off for a while."

Riley also hears them, and her drink pauses halfway to her mouth. She looks at me over her sunglasses and motions towards the women talking. I only nod.

Maybe they're talking about something else entirely, and I'm reading into it.

Bull shit. I know it's the same woman we saw earlier.

And I'm pretty sure she's dead.

Goddammit.

I squeeze my eyes shut for a second, willing that thought away. First, the man at dinner, now this? This is supposed to be a vacation, not a floating crime scene.

I lean over and whisper in Riley's ear. "I still say we don't tell them."

She flips her head around to gape at me. "Seriously?" She asks after a beat.

I nod. "Seriously. Why upset them?"

"Because it seems like, from what we are hearing, that another person has died on this boat. They should know." She protests.

"All it's going to do is upset everyone, and this is supposed to be a fun trip to celebrate Andrea."

"What are you two whispering about over there?" Andrea slurs at us.

Riley gives me a long look, the hesitation apparent in her eyes, but sighs and turns to Andrea. "Lexi is trying to convince me that her margaritas are better than my Long Islands."

"Margaritas will always win." Sean holds his up in solidarity.

Pointing at him, I laugh. "That's why you're such a keeper."

Andrea and Riley roll their eyes in unison.

***

Thankfully, dinner tonight isn't as eventful as last night's. We get a table quickly and have our food in front of us before we know it.

Two men, one younger and one older, dressed in matching elegant attire, are roaming around the dining room. Neither of them has sat down, and they are slyly looking over all the diners at their tables.

If you look hard enough, you can spot them as security.

I'm just going to believe they always do this, and I'm only paranoid because of earlier.

"I still say we do our own thing," Claire's voice cuts into my thoughts. "We can rent some Jeeps and go explore."

Right. We're planning our day in Mexico tomorrow, and I try to focus again.

"Why can't we just get one of those island passes and sit on the beach drinking all day?" George suggests.

"I want to swim with dolphins," Riley whines and pouts at me.

We all look around at each other.

"We're splitting up for the day, aren't we?" I sigh.

"Looks like it!" Andrea nods.

Sean looks at everyone, looking a little less green than he has been so far this trip. "I think I would rather go to the ruins. So maybe Jeeps would be a good idea."

Once it's settled that we're splitting, I can't help but smile that Riley and I will be spending the day together. All because I am a sucker and can't say no to her, even if swimming with dolphins wasn't on my to-do list.

"What about the rest of tonight?" Hannah asks, eyes brighter than they were the previous day. "A murder-mystery game starts and goes through the rest of the cruise. You have to look for clues and things like that to solve it."

Riley and I share a look while everyone else agrees it sounds fun.

"Lex," Andrea nudges my leg under the table. "You good?" She squints and studies me.

I plaster a smile on my face. "Yeah, that sounds like it could be interesting."

"Let's finish up so we can go get good seats. It starts in about 30 minutes."

We finish our drinks and desserts and then go to the Main Theater.

***

"Murder. Mystery. Who will be the one to figure out the killer before the cruise is over?" The Cruise Director says in a suspenseful tone.

Honestly, I'd rather swim with the sharks than be here in this theater.

Between last night and today, I want no part of anything having to do with death. The rest of the group seems excited though, so I'll be toughing it out.

"This game is not a race, but a challenge of your mind to find clues, solve them, and by the end of this amazing cruise, decide who *YOU* believe is the killer." The host goes on to explain. "Those you see on stage with me are only a few of the cast that are a part of the game. The rest may be hidden in places you will be led to by your clues."

The cast on stage shoots each other suspicious looks, playing into the characters.

"I will tell you that one of the lovely people on stage with me is a murderer. But who could it be?" He smiles so big in glee that his entire face scrunches up. "It's your job to find out before the rest of them end up dead."

I wince and fidget in my seat. The bluntness about death is starting to get under my skin.

"Questioning people is part of the game, and the crew members are all aware. If a crew member tells you they do not have a clue or are not a part of the game, please do not harass them, as they are telling the truth. Those who are playing have to disclose that they are involved."

"Wanna be good cop or bad cop?" Riley teases as she sidles up next to me. "I'd prefer to be bad cop, but I can share."

Jesus. Fucking. Christ.

After explaining the rules, we split into duos to solve the crime instead of working as one giant group. We also decided it would be more fun to be paired up with someone other than a significant other. Andrea ends up with George, Sean with Hannah, Claire with Riley, and I'm with Pru.

We all stand after we've been dismissed to make our way to our new partner and get our first clue.

"Alright, friend," Pru rubs her hands together. "Out of everyone here, you and I have this."   She scans the room. "Who gives off the creepiest vibe?"

I bark out a laugh. "Literally everyone we have met so far," I joke, only partially serious.

Pru rolls her eyes as we get to our clue:

Bright lights, it's your ticket to fame,

10 and 11 should be your aim,

You can't lose if you have nothing to gain.

"Are you kidding me?" Pru groans. "I take back what I said earlier. This is all on you."

Great. There have been possibly two actual deaths on this cruise, and now we're playing pretend like nothing ever happened. How the fuck are we supposed to just go about this game looking for a "murderer" when I'm beginning to think that there's possibly an actual murderer on board with us, hiding in wait for the next victim?

Chapter Six

Waves crashed on the shore of the secluded beach, the sun shining brightly on the sand as birds cawed above. The couple chose this area because of the peacefulness, as there were no other people or sounds of passing cars.

They knew that going onto a beach with a *No Trespassing* sign was risky, but wanting to escape to their own little paradise had made them throw caution to the wind. The fact that the beach was off-limits only heightened the excitement of being alone.

Their rented Jeep was parked hidden behind a dune as they laughed, playing in the shallow waves together.

Their belongings were carelessly thrown on their towels on the beach; there was no need to worry about anyone taking them, as no one else was around. They were able to enjoy their private oasis without any care.

Coming up from being dunked once again, the man noticed a figure on the beach rifling through their things. He hadn't even seen them approach—it was almost like they had materialized out of thin air.

"Hey! What the hell are you doing?" He shouted from the water, his voice cutting through the peaceful quiet. The woman with him whipped around to see what he was yelling at.

"This is a private beach," the stranger straightened and said with no emotion as they stood and stared at them.

Their voice was monotone, and the couple looked on in disbelief as the stranger watched them with blank eyes.

They shared a glance before the woman hollered, "Get the fuck out of here!"

She began to tread out of the water, making her way towards the intruder; her steps were sure and angry, but they lost speed as she got closer.

The person on the beach smiled, a slow, deliberate grin.

Eerily calm.

"Babe..." her partner said hesitantly from the water, unease passing through him as the stranger watched her approach.

She didn't answer but slowed her pace, unnerved by the figure standing there in stillness, watching her. "I don't know what your deal is, jackass, but we'll leave if it's that big of a deal to you. Just leave our shit alone." She had reached their towels and paused to stare at the stranger before she bent down to grab her purse.

The newcomer moved as fast as lightning.

They grabbed her hair and pulled her head back violently. The blade that had suddenly appeared glinted in the blinding sunlight as it ran over her throat.

She cried out, her body going rigid, but it was too late; her life quickly ended with the white sand stained red from her blood.

The man in the water screamed in agony as he splashed out of the water and ran towards her, calling her name.

"I told you," the voice said with an edge of playfulness, "*This is a private beach.*"

The woman's partner fell to his knees beside her and sobbed as he tried to stop the bleeding.   His hands were trembling.

There was so much blood. It covered everything, and the man gagged at the sight of it.

"No, no, no." He cried out in panic, staring at his hands, trying to wipe the blood on his wet shorts when it wouldn't stop.

The killer behind him watched for a beat, smiling, savoring, and then plunged the same knife into the back of the grieving man's neck.

This cruise was supposed to be a celebration—fun before their lives started—and now it was over.

His body trembled, his mind racing, but the world faded to nothing before he could understand that his future had ended when they stepped on this beach.

CHAPTER SEVEN

We wake early the next day, as the ship starts disembarking at 8:00 a.m. for our day in Mexico. The night before, we had decided to meet and explore the central part of Cozumel before going our separate ways for the day.

Hannah is leaning on the wall and frowns. "Can't we just stay on the ship? I'm sure it will be nice and quiet with everyone leaving."

"Absolutely not." George squeezes her softly as he puts an arm around her shoulders. "We can skip the next one if you really want to."

We're all crowded in a stairwell, waiting to get through the checkpoint before being let off to roam free. I am starting to side with Hannah on staying behind on the ship, as the woman behind me keeps hitting me with her bag.

I'm close to losing my shit, and I have to keep reminding myself to breathe and that we're all stuck in here together with nowhere else to move.

"I'm so excited to swim with the dolphins." Riley is lit up like a fucking Christmas tree, and I fondly watch as she runs a hand through her wavy hair. The ocean air is definitely doing great things for it.

We finally make it off the boat, shockingly without me grabbing the bag from the woman behind me and beating her with it. The sun beams down on us as we leisurely walk towards the central area of Cozumel. The smell of the salt water mixed with the scent wafting from the local restaurants immediately makes me regret skipping breakfast.

Andrea and Riley walk ahead while I hang back with Pru and Hannah. The guys stop to look in a surf shop, and Claire decides to stop at a boutique to browse sundresses. I lose sight of Dre and Riley while we wait for the others.

"I am ready for some sun and some margaritas," Pru looks around, dancing happily from one foot to the next.

"I still wish I had stayed behind," Hannah laments. "I am so tired and could use a day of doing nothing."

"That's what yesterday was for." I can't help but laugh. "You were the one who wanted to stay up late hunting down clues."

"Oh!" Hannah perks up. "Did you figure out your first clue?"

Pru and I, in fact, did not figure out our first clue. Instead, we found a bar and watched everyone else scramble to figure out theirs while we drank our margaritas.

"Like we'd tell you if we did. You're competition." I joke, sharing a sneaky smile with Pru.

Suddenly, a Styrofoam container appears before me as Riley and Andrea reappear. "Don't say I never gave you anything," Riley jokes.

I arch a brow as I take it and open it. My senses are immediately flooded with the smell of fresh pastry and cinnamon, and my mouth waters at the sight of fresh churros coated in caramel. "I love you." I sigh happily and dig in.

I don't notice Riley tense next to me.

Andrea rolls her eyes. "It will be noon by the time these boys take their 'quick look'. What time do your excursions leave?" she asks the rest of us.

Pru looks at her watch. "We have to meet at the rental place in 15 minutes. I'm going to hunt Claire down. We'll meet you in the Atrium at six for dinner."

"Sounds like a plan." Hannah nods in agreement.

"We'd better head over to our bus, too," Riley says and shoots me an endearing look, my cheeks full of churro. "If I miss the dolphins, this cruise will have been for nothing."

"Thanks, Rye." Andrea deadpans.

***

Taking our seats on the bus, I gave my last churro to Riley, who was practically vibrating in her seat with excitement. We found an open bench near the back of the bus and settled in for the 30-minute drive to the dolphin sanctuary.

"So, where was your clue last night?" Riley asks, licking her fingers. I gulp as I try not to stare blatantly as her tongue wraps around them.

"Uh..." It takes my brain a second to catch up. "We didn't find it."

"What? How?" She scoffs.

"We got distracted by the call of margaritas?" I give a cheeky grin.

Riley rolls her eyes. "Ours was at the cafe. Our second clue sucks, though. I have no idea what it means."

"Can't be worse than our first one," I remember how ridiculous ours was. "What is it?"

She shakes her head. "No way. If you can't even bother to play, I'm not including you." She sticks her tongue out at me.

I shrug and look out the window as I watch the scenery pass. The blue sky and green grass stretch out for miles on one side, the ocean peeking over the dunes as we pass on the other. It's gorgeous and a welcome change from the buildings and mountain life back home.

My mind goes to where I don't want it, and I begin to think about everything that has happened so far this cruise. I want to believe the past two days were just flukes, but I can't shake this unease that it's not all copasetic.

"Hey, Rye." I turn to her. "Do you think it's weird that two people have died?" I ask quietly.

Riley frowns and thinks for a moment. "Lex, shit happens. That dude had a heart attack, which is sadly just a normal medical emergency. I have no idea about the woman, and we don't even know for a fact if she died. She could have been super drunk and needed to sleep it off." She reasons, and I don't know if she's trying to convince me or herself.

"But that towel was soaked in blood. The whole area was closed off for the day."

"Babe, we don't know what happened, and I doubt we'll ever find out. If she did die, we have no idea why. I think it's best to let it go and continue on with our cruise."

"James seemed to be able to find out about the man from dinner. What can he find out about the woman?" I ask.

"They gave James privileges that night with the man because they were a doctor short due to another emergency. I doubt they'll tell him anything about the woman." Riley explains.

I nod without saying anything and drop it for now, and we fall into silence, as I don't want to bring down Riley's excitement.

We finally make it to our destination with only one near miss, as these people in Cozumel drive like fucking maniacs. Riley hops off the bus and squeals at the open water spanning in front of us.

"Did you know that dolphins can talk to each other and give each other names?" She whips around with a happy glint in her eye.

"I did not know that," I confirm, matching her smile.

"They also use other animals for pleasuring themselves."

I gawk. "That I didn't need to know." I shake my head and try to get those images out of my mind. "And why do you want to swim with these things?"

She rolls her eyes dramatically, her mouth twitching, fighting a smile. "Because they're majestic as fuck, that's why." She turns around to follow the others who have started walking away.

We make it to the shore and grab the snorkeling gear that the crew passes out to everyone. We then go through a brief lecture on what to do and especially what *not* to do when we get in the water. Apparently, other animals are not the only thing that dolphins use to get themselves off, and I definitely regret that I agreed to this.

But then I look at my best friend, and my heart melts. She has her snorkel gear on and is ready to go, her smile brighter than the sun beating down on us.

I love her.

There's no denying it anymore.

I am in love with this dork.

"Lex!" Riley giggles happily. "Let's go find a new friend."

***

We did find a new friend, and a few more after that. Thankfully, the dolphins behaved themselves, and I escaped unscathed.

At the end of our time, Riley demanded that we take pictures with a dolphin named Cricket, and she dragged me into the shot with them. Once the excursion was over, we went into a hut to look at the pictures we had taken.

I study the picture a little too long, but I can't resist. Riley's hair is curled from the water, and she has a radiant smile as she holds onto the dolphin. In it, I'm staring at her instead of the camera like the lovesick fool I am.

Riley gives me a look like she knows exactly what I am thinking before I give her a playful shove and put the picture in my bag.

We're still wet and sticky from the water on the bus back to the port. I feel alive with the salt on my skin and my hair dripping down my back. It was a great day. Swimming with carefree and playful animals helped alleviate the tension growing inside me.

We decide to find food before heading back to the ship, and we run into Pru, Claire, George, and Hannah at one of the restaurants. "Hey!" I chirp, surprised that we found them in the mass of people around. "Where are Andrea and Sean?" I look around.

George shrugs. "I have no idea. We ran into these two after Hannah started to get super hungry. Dre and Sean ended up doing their own thing."

"No doubt they wanted some private beach time," Claire wiggles her eyebrows.

"Gross, Claire!" I crinkle my nose in disgust. "Has anyone tried to text them? Our phones work in Mexico, don't they?"

The group looks at each other and then back at me. "I can try." Hannah reaches into her bag for her phone.

Riley adds two chairs to the table and motions for me to sit. "They're fine. We still have two hours before the ship leaves," she reassures me, voice strong and sure. "Now feed me. I'm hungry."

Pru's eyes watch between me and Riley, giving me an unreadable look before changing the subject. "So, there was this woman who got insanely drunk at the tequila tasting we did," she starts. "By the time we left, her husband and another guy were having to carry her back to the jeep, and when she sat down, her tit was just hanging out of her shirt."

"No way!" Riley gasps, head thrown back in a laugh.

"Yes way." Claire snorts. "It was just sitting there, flopping along when they left. Her husband looked so fed up and didn't even try to cover her."

I smile, but I can't help but start worrying—the doubts from earlier are beginning to creep back in. I thought Dre and Sean would go with Pru and Claire to explore. I didn't know they were going off alone, or I would have told her to meet us sooner than dinner tonight.

I try to push it to the back of my mind and try to enjoy lunch with the rest of the group.

Then I hear that woman's screams from the first night in my mind.

I see the woman we thought was passed out on the deck.

"Have you heard from Andrea?" I cut Riley off mid-sentence to ask Hannah.

Hannah checks her phone. "Nothing yet. I'm sure they're fine. There's a lot to do here."

The unease finally wins, overshadowing the lighthearted fun we are all having together. "I'm going back to the boat to check if they're back. Does anyone remember their cabin number?" I look around as I stand up.

Everyone shakes their head.

Fuck.

My fingers tremble as I reach for my phone, and I walk away, but Riley's hand stops me, warm and firm against mine. "Lexi, stop for a second," she says calmly. "There's no telling where they are right now. They could still be out and about, or they could be anywhere on the boat." She steps closer, looks me deeply in the eye, and squeezes my hand reassuringly. "Dre is fine. Please sit back down and eat with us, and then I will help you find her."

We stand there, eyes locked, the tension thick between us. I want to trust her, fuck, I know I should, but my anxiety keeps me rooted to the spot. It's not just about Andrea anymore; it's about everything happening between me and Riley, too, and I can't figure out how to wrap my head around any of it.

Finally, I nod, defeated.

***

Riley throws some cash on the table and gets up after eating. "We'll see you guys at six. We're going to go find them, so this one," she hooks her thumb at me, "will chill the fuck out."

I glare at the brunette.

We walk quickly back to the ship, and I curse at how far away it feels. Riley keeps the pace next to me, talking a mile a minute. I know she's trying to keep me calm, but I can't help but feel like I'm suffocating.

I spin toward Riley, my frustration bubbling over. "Babe, I know you're trying to help, but it's not working." Riley frowns and looks at me in concern. "Can we please just focus on getting to the boat?"

"Lex, take a breath." She throws her arm around me and starts to walk again, keeping me close to her side. "I know things have been weird this cruise, but I need you to breathe."

I didn't realize how much her presence would ground me and how much I craved it.

By the time we reach the ship, I feel a little less on edge, but the worry is still there, making my head hurt.

When I check my phone and see no notifications, I feel defeated and sit in the first chair I see. "It's no use. I don't know where they are." My head drops into my hands as I lean over and take a deep breath.

Riley looks around and sits next to me. Putting her hand on my back, she rubs gently. "Let's look around the Lido Deck, and if we don't find them there, we can go to guest services and see if we can get their room number."

I look up at her and give her a small smile. "That's a good idea. Thank you."

She nods once, and we stand, heading to the main deck and taking a lap around it.

No Andrea. No Sean.

We get in line at guest services, and Riley taps away on her phone while we wait. "Did you get ahold of them?" I ask, hopeful.

"No, it's James." Riley doesn't look up as she keeps tapping the screen.

Of course it's fucking James. I'm about to have a nervous break-down, and she's getting texts from the guy who won't go away.

"What the fuck does he want?" It's out of my mouth before I can stop it.

She raises a brow as she looks up from her phone. "He was just seeing how my day went. Why?" She asks defensively.

I only shake my head and brush it off. I don't have time to worry about that as we reach the front of the line.

The woman behind the counter appears to want to be anywhere else. "How can I help you?"

"Hi. I'm looking for my sister, and I can't remember what room she is in. Can you look it up?" I ask, hopeful.

"No can do. We can't give out private information." The woman pops her gum, staring blankly at us.

Take a deep breath, Lexi...

"Look," Riley cuts in, her tone sharp. "We can't reach them, and we're worried." Her eyes are flashing, and I can tell she is about to lose all patience with this woman.

She looks at Riley disinterestedly. "I can't give out their room number, but I can try to page them over the intercom if you are that concerned." In dismissal, she focuses back on her screen.

Anger, taking the place of frustration, has me slamming my hand onto the desk before I can stop myself. "I'm not just asking for no reason," I snap, my voice cracking. "I'm asking because something's wrong, and I can feel it." My fists clench on the desk, the words spilling out before I can stop them. "Page them."

In shock, Riley stands beside me, and the crew member reaches for something before looking back up at me, glaring. "You need to calm down."

We stare each other down, and an older security officer appears the next moment.

"Ma'am, I need you to step over here with me," he says with authority and a harsh look in my direction.

"You called security?" Riley scoffs at the woman. "Are you kidding me?"

The man points at Riley and nods in the direction of a hallway. "Both of you. Come with me."

We follow him like scolded children. My heart is racing, and I reach for Riley's hand without thinking, gripping it tightly as I try to calm myself down.

"Alright." We step away from other passengers, and the officer looks between us. "I'm   Keith," he introduces himself. "Can you tell me what's wrong?"

"I'm just trying to figure out my sister's cabin number to check on her." My voice shakes as I try to calm down and let the anger cool off.

Keith's brow furrows. "Why do you need to check on her?"

Riley glances at me out of the corner of her eye. "She's worried that something happened to her because she can't get in touch with her."

"When was the last time you saw her? Was she supposed to be somewhere?" He grabs a notepad out of his back pocket. "How old is she?"

I grimace. "We went our separate ways earlier today, and I haven't heard from her." Standing before this man, I feel a wave of embarrassment. Maybe I am overreacting for no reason. "She's my older sister. We're supposed to meet at six for dinner."

Keith sighs, and the hand with the notebook drops to his side. "So, there is no indication that anything is wrong?"

Under his gaze, I feel like I'm two feet tall. Riley steps forward, and like the anchor she is, she places a grounding hand on my arm above where our hands are still intertwined.

The notebook returns to his pocket, and Keith holds his hands out before him. "I'm sorry, but if there's no reason to think that something has happened to her, there's nothing I can help with. She's an adult." He looks at his watch. "Everyone should be headed back to the ship now. I'm sure she'll show up with everyone else."

He doesn't understand. He can't understand.

"What about the two people who have died so far this cruise. Is that not enough cause for concern?" I press, the anger flaring back up.

Riley closes her eyes and takes a deep breath while the officer gives me a warning look. "Ma'am, those-"

"It's Lexi," I interrupt.

"Lexi," he nods. "Those were medical emergencies. I can't give more information, but there is nothing suspicious about either one." He looks between me and Riley and sighs. "Look, I get it," his voice softens. "But we can't break protocol. We'll figure it out if she doesn't show up for dinner and you come back here. But I can't do anything for you now."

What more can I say to get him to realize something is wrong? No one is listening to me. How do I even explain a gut feeling without coming across even crazier? Especially now that he confirmed that the woman did die.

"There's really nothing you can do?" I deflate, but I'm not ready to give up. "You can't check on her right now?"

Keith shakes his head. "There's no reason to. I'm sorry. I need to get downstairs and ensure everything gets closed before we disembark."

All of a sudden, his radio crackles to life. "Security, priority two on deck 0."

"Come on, Lex," Riley says gently. "We can grab a drink, hang out on the deck, and see if we run into them."

The last thing on my mind is drinking, but I know Riley is trying to help by distracting me. I appreciate it and hate it at the same time.

"Okay." I exhale slowly. "Alright."

"Please make sure to be respectful if you do have to come back later." Keith gives me a pointed look.

I blush. "Yes, sir."

Keith gives us both one last look before sauntering off to the lower decks, and Riley and I are left standing there staring at each other.

She sighs. "Come on. Let's play nice and have that bitch at guest services page them."

She offers me a smile, and I slightly relax at the sight.

CHAPTER EIGHT

After Keith left, we returned to guest services with sheepish smiles. The woman at the desk, whose name we found out was Linda, while unhappy, did page Andrea and Sean, and we waited for 15 minutes before giving up.

We end up on the Lido Deck, sitting where we can watch people reboarding the ship. I scan every face we see, and none are Andrea or Sean. We finally spot the rest of the gang, though, and we holler down to them and wave until they look up at us. They join us with fresh drinks once they make it through the checkpoint.

I check my watch, my heart pounding in time with the ticking seconds. "What time are we supposed to leave tonight?" I wonder out loud, already knowing the answer.

George glances at Hannah, and something uneasy flickers between them. "Five," he says, his voice low.

It's 5:15.

"Guys..." I inhale a shaky breath. "I don't like this. Where are they?"

They are still calling for Andrea and Sean on the loudspeakers, as well as two other names.

My stomach churns. I'm going to be sick. I tell the group as much, then stand abruptly and make a beeline for the bathroom. Riley's right behind me, slipping into the stall before I can shut the door.

"Rye—"

"Shut up and let me hold your hair," she says firmly, crouching beside me as I drop to the cold floor and heave into the toilet.

***

Once I've emptied my stomach, we regroup and agree to meet in the Atrium at six, as we had planned earlier in the day.

I want to wait near the Atrium, knowing Dre is always early, but Riley refuses to let me. "You need to get out of your bathing suit and wet clothes," she admonishes me, touching my wrist and walking backward toward our cabin, beckoning me to come with her. "And you need to freshen up. Please, it'll make you feel better." Her voice holds promise that I try, and fail, to believe.

We're quiet as we get to the cabin, and I quickly do as Riley instructed. I change into something appropriate for dinner, brush my teeth and wash my face, and fifteen minutes later, we are out the door and on our way to meet everyone.

Riley looks ridiculously hot in a sparkly low-cut top and short shorts, and my anxiety is so bad that I can't even appreciate it. At this point, I'm basically dragging her through the ship as we head to the meeting spot.

No one is there yet, and my shoulders hunch.

"Hey."

Andrea.

I whip around and there they are. Both of them. Like they haven't been *missing* all damn day. Like I didn't spiral into a full-blown breakdown.

My eyes fill with tears, and I grab Dre in a bear hug. She yelps at the intensity of the hug and pats me on the back awkwardly. "Ouch," she mutters in my ear as she tries to break the hug.

I pull away from her and immediately punch her in the shoulder.

"Ow!" She protests loudly, and her hand goes to her shoulder protectively. "What the fuck, Lexi?"

Before anyone can say anything else, Riley almost bowls her over with a hug of her own. Sean watches, wide-eyed.

"Where the fuck have you been?" I demand. "Do you have any idea how worried I was?"

Andrea takes a step back and looks between me and Riley. "Sean started freaking out about missing the ship and getting stuck, so we came back early and ended up falling asleep." She says sheepishly, but shares a look with Sean that I don't know how to decipher.

He won't meet my eyes, and I realize I don't think I want to know why they came back early.

"You can't just disappear like that! Did you not hear them calling your names over the loudspeakers?" I press a hand to my chest and try to breathe. "You have *no idea* what I went through."

Andrea comes up and gives me a soft hug. "You could have come and knocked on the door."

"We couldn't remember your room number," Riley says.

"It's 7234," Sean announces. "I'm sorry we made you worry."

Made me worry—like I haven't been literally sick over this. Like tossing out a room number now makes it all okay. Like today didn't happen.

"I think I need to go lie down." I shake my head, the adrenaline dump making me exhausted. "I'll grab food later," I tell Riley when I see her open her mouth to protest. "You guys enjoy your dinner. I'll meet up with you."

I look between the three of them before I walk away. As I walk toward the cabin, I run into Pru and Claire, who I ignore as they call out to me.

I need to lie down. I need to figure out what the hell is going on with me.

***

I pace and glance at the clock. Riley hasn't responded to my messages in over an hour. She had told me that she was going to get a drink with James, making my heart drop against my will.

Not hearing from her feels like déjà vu, and I cannot handle another round of someone 'missing'. Last I had heard, everyone was resting after dinner and planning to meet in the casino at nine.

Riley was supposed to come here first, and it's now 8:55.

While I was decompressing in the room, the ship finally departed the port. They kept making announcements for two passengers to report to guest services, and I'm guessing we were waiting on them before setting sail.

As I'm pondering this, the cabin door suddenly bursts open, and Riley walks in with a smile. I'm across the room before I can think, grabbing her by the arms. She freezes, wide-eyed.

"Where the fuck have you been?" I demand. "You haven't responded to any of my messages."

"I told you I went to get a drink." Riley pulls out of my tight grip and rubs her arm. "One drink turned into three. I'm sorry I didn't check in with you, Mom." She rolls her eyes as she goes to the mirror and checks her eye makeup.

"I was worried something happened to you," I whisper, looking at my hands. "Did you not think about what happened with Dre earlier?"

Riley arches an eyebrow and stares at me through the mirror. "Lexi, what the fuck is going on with you?"

I sigh and sit on the edge of the bed. "I don't know. I think I'm just wound up from the day, I'm so worried that something will happen to one of you."

"So that's your problem?" She scoffs.

I scrunch my nose. "What do you mean. Yes, that's my problem."

Riley sighs heavily and shakes her head. "Of course. What else could it be?" She mutters to herself, but I hear her.

"What are you talking about?" I ask, confused.

Riley throws her hands up. "I don't know. Maybe it's the fact that you've been making comments about James since we met him?" She glares.

"What does that even have to do with anything?" I snap.

She rolls her eyes and grasps the bottom of her shirt, pulling it over her head. "Never mind. Forget I said anything." She throws the shirt in the corner and reaches into a drawer to grab a t-shirt.

I hop off the bed and make my way over to the brunette. "Rye, what the hell is going on?"

Riley slams the drawer closed and whirls to face me.

"You don't fucking get it! You never have!"

"I've never gotten what?" My fists clench by my side, and I explode. "I can't read your fucking mind!"

Riley throws her T-shirt to the floor and strides up to me, grabbing my face with both hands and crashing her lips onto mine. The kiss is anything but gentle—tongue, teeth, desperation. I freeze for half a second, stunned, and then my brain catches up. My arms go around her, and I kiss her back with everything I've got.

Her hand slides to the back of my neck, deepening the kiss. "You're such a fucking idiot," she gasps into my mouth.

I pull back far enough to look and stare her in the eye. "Riley..."

"I'm in love with you," she says, her voice cracking with emotion. "How the fuck have you not picked up on that?"

Her words hit me right in the heart.

Holy fuck.

This time, I'm the one who moves first. I surge forward and crash my lips against hers in a bruising kiss. She lets out a choked, relieved sob as she kisses me back. I spin us around and push her down onto the bed, our mouths never parting as we fall together onto the soft mattress.

I rest my weight on her, and her arms wrap around me tightly to lock me in place. Tongues intertwined, I cradle her cheek with one hand. She tastes like rum and everything I've ever dreamed of.

Her legs come up, wrapping around my waist, pulling me in as I rock forward, and she arches to meet me. "Lexi," she gasps and rolls her hips into mine.

I groan and grind again. I can feel the heat radiating off her skin and remember that she is only in her bra.

This. This is everything I have ever wanted.

Riley. Here with me like this.

I lift my head, breaking the heated kiss. "Rye..." I place a chaste kiss on her lips. "Why didn't you tell me?"

"Can we talk about this later?" she murmurs, her fingers skimming the hem of my shirt as her hips arch up again.

"We really should talk, " I say, sitting up. Her hands pull my shirt over my head, cutting off any train of thought.

Her hands immediately find my stomach, nails raking down my bare skin and leaving fire in their wake. I shiver before I pull her into a sitting position so I can reach behind her to unhook her bra.

Bam, bam, bam.

We both whip around to look at the door, and Riley falls back, groaning and putting her hands over her face.

"What the fuck," she bemoans.

"Hey bitches, open up!" Pru calls from the other side of the door. "It's 9:30 and we have gambling to do!"

I sigh heavily as I lean over Riley again, gently kissing her lips.

I stand up and find my shirt, putting it back on as Riley sits up and pouts. I start walking to the door, but I turn back once I get there and meet her eyes.

"We will finish this later," I reassure her.

Riley beams.

CHAPTER NINE

Riley gets off the bed, snatches her T-shirt off the floor, and goes into the bathroom after placing another quick kiss on my lips. I fling the cabin door open once she is hidden behind the bathroom door.

"Are you kidding me right now?" I ask Andrea and Pru, my voice low and threatening.

Andrea looks past me into the room. "I'm sorry, are we interrupting something?" she asks cheekily.

"I will kill you with my bare hands." I hiss as Riley steps out of the bathroom, fully dressed, and pauses when she sees me and Andrea in the middle of a stare-down.

"I'm not even going to ask," Riley announces, pushing past me into the hall. "Let's go win some money!"

***

The slot machines' bright lights, loud noises, and raucous laughter, which float throughout the room, bring new life to the group.

I don't know if it's the contagious energy or what happened with Riley earlier, hell, maybe it's a mix of both, but I'm feeling good now.

As we join the rest of the group, Claire immediately grabs Riley and pulls her away. We share a secretive look before she allows herself to be dragged off to God knows where.

"Claire said their next clue is about the casino." Pru comes up next to me. "Let's figure out our clue."

Right. The murder-mystery game. I had almost forgotten about that.

I guess that happens when real life feels more like a murder mystery than the game does.

I try not to think about that as I recall the less-than-helpful clue we had the night before.

Gasping suddenly, I smack Pru on the arm. "Blackjack!"

Pru's eyes go wide, and she nods. We head to the Blackjack tables. "Which one?" She asks.

I study each table, then point. "That one."

We see a table with a $100 buy-in and no one sitting there, and we plop into empty seats as the dealer warily looks at us.

"Hi. Our clue led us here." Pru grins sweetly. "Please tell me you have our next one."

The dealer rolls his eyes. "I should have known that you weren't coming to, oh, I don't know, play the actual game I'm running." He hands us a piece of paper. "Congratulations," he deadpans as we high-five and stand up, leaving without a second glance.

We open the paper:

I'll be where the sun shines,

Whatever you do, don't forget the lime,

If you're lucky, you won't spend a dime.

"That has to be a bar, right?" Pru guesses, and I nod in agreement. "Great, 'cause there aren't a million of those," she frowns.

Claire and Riley show up just then, grinning like they won a million bucks.

"I take it you found the next clue?" Pru asks, wraps her arm around Claire, and presses a kiss to the side of her head.

Riley smirks at me and winks.

My heart skips a beat.

"I want to play the slots," Riley says, giving me a pointed look. "Want to come with me?"

"You bet." I agree quickly, leaving Pru and Claire to discuss the murder-mystery clues.

I follow Riley around as she looks like she is on a mission. I'm about to ask her what she's looking for when I notice we're in the back of the casino, tucked away in a corner. She leans against the wall with a smirk and crooks her finger at me.

"Come here," she husks.

Who am I to say no?

I walk over and stop right in front of her. "Is there something you needed?" I raise a playful eyebrow.

Riley hooks her fingers in my belt loops and pulls my body against hers. "Yeah. You." She says before she kisses me.

The rush from earlier comes back immediately as soon as her lips touch mine. For once, I'm not questioning anything.

I'm just here with her.

We stand in the corner, hidden from our friends, making out like horny teenagers before she pries her lips from mine and pushes me back.

"Okay, we'd better stop before someone comes looking for us," she frowns. "Again."

I laugh and nod. "Come on, let's go find some slots to play."

***

"Goddammit." Riley pouts as her machine spins and lands on nothing again.

Suppressing a giggle, I gently rub her thigh. "You're really not having any luck tonight."

"Oh yeah?" She challenges. "I wouldn't say that's completely true." She wiggles her eyebrows at me.

"You're in my seat."

A deep voice behind me makes me jump, and I turn to look over my shoulder, confused. "There was no one here when I sat down," I explain with a shrug.

Riley looks between us and then reaches for my hand. "We can move," she tells the man, and I turn to her with a questioning look.

I realize that the man looks familiar, and it hits me that it's the douchebag from the first day who cut in front of us at the bar.

I hit the spin button again, and suddenly, the lights start flashing, and a loud noise erupts from my machine. I watch as the 'free spins' feature activates, and then the money counter starts climbing.

"Holy shit!" I exclaim, in shock, as the number keeps getting higher.

"That's my money." The man growls and puts a hand on my shoulder.

Riley bolts up out of her seat, her posture suddenly defensive, muscles tensing as she shoves the man back. She plants her feet, and

I stare at them in shock. "Back the fuck up, dick," Riley's voice drops an octave.

I hear the bartender from the bar calling security on their radio.

"That's my machine. Which means that's my money." He growls and comes at Riley, who drops her shoulder and plows right into him.

He stumbles back, a shocked look on his face, before it twists into anger. He lunges again at Riley, who quickly bypasses him.

Suddenly, I hear voices shouting as the rest of our group runs up to us. Sean and George are angrier than I have ever seen them.

Sean is about to go for the man when a security guard comes rushing in and pushes him aside. The officer grabs the man's arm and twists it behind his back, and I realize it is the same officer from our encounter earlier this evening.

Another, younger security guard rushes up to us. "Are you okay?" he asks me, and I nod dumbly as he grabs Riley. Riley tries to wrestle her arm out of his grasp, and suddenly, I wonder if they're here to help us.

"Lexi," Keith recognizes and acknowledges me. "Care to explain what is going on?"

"We were sitting here, minding our business playing, and this asshat said it was his machine." Riley glares at the offender and wrenches her arm from the younger officer's grasp. "We didn't do anything."

The officer goes for Riley again, but Keith shakes his head. "Let her go, Theodore."

"All I saw was you shoving this guy," Theodore says, looking at all of us.

Pru and Hannah protectively stand on either side of Riley and glare at this new officer.

"Lexi!" Andrea rushes to stand next to me. "What the hell is going on?"

"Everything is fine," I reassure her.

Keith looks at me and motions towards Dre. "Your sister?"

I nod, and the machine behind me dings loudly, drawing our attention.

"Come on, buddy." Keith pulls up on the arm in his grasp, making the man wince. "Let's go talk."

Theodore raises a brow at the machine and looks between us. "Congrats on your win," he nods at me, then follows Keith.

"What in the world just happened?" Andrea demands.

"Well," Riley drawls. "It looks like Lex just won $1,300." She laughs and smirks at me.

Well, hasn't this day turned from a nightmare into one unexpected surprise after the next?

"Yeah, I think I'm done on that note." I hit the cash-out button and grabbed the slip of paper as an attendant arrived with paperwork for me to fill out.

Once I have completed the necessary paperwork for my win, I turn to the group. "Is anyone hungry?" My stomach reminds me that I never ate earlier.

"Come on, big shot," Riley loops her arm in mine. "Let's get you some food."

***

"I can't believe you squared up to that guy. He was twice your size." I chide Riley around a mouthful of cheese pizza.

After the casino debacle, the boys said pizza sounded good, so we found the pizza stand and a table on the outside deck to eat at.

"How did that cop know I was your sister?" Andrea inquires with a raised brow.

I blush and cough. "Uhh. There might have been an incident earlier, and he got called over it."

Dre closes her eyes and sighs. "Lex, at the beginning of this cruise, I told you I would blame you if anything went wrong."

My mouth falls open. "Nothing this trip has been my fault!" I look around at everyone. "In fact, everyone message your room numbers in the chat right now so we all know in case this happens again." I glower at my sister.

No one protests as they message so that we all have a reference in case it's needed.

"So, what's the plan for tomorrow? We never booked any excursions," Sean mentions. "Do we want to stay behind, drink, and party on the ship? Or go into the city and shop for a little?"

"Whatever you decide to do, I'm going with you," I tell him. "We are not separating again."

"Where you go, I go!" Riley smiles at me, and my cheeks heat up.

"I think that's a great idea," Hannah chimes in. "I'm not really feeling a huge excursion."

"I'm down with all that, but we are not missing zip lining in Ocho Rios." Pru insists.

"Yes!" Riley and Pru high-five over the table.

George looks up from his phone. "If we're not waking up early, there's a late-night comedy show that starts at 11:30. We can grab seats when Lex is done stuffing her face."

I scowl around another mouthful of pizza. "Fuck you."

***

The comedy show proves to be a good idea. Hannah's mood has turned around, and she is laughing and smiling more than she has during this whole trip. The rest of the group hoots and howls with laughter at the comedian while I relax for the first time in what feels like ages.

A hand appears on my thigh under the table and starts to rub up and down slowly. I gulp as my body immediately heats up.

"Do you think they'd notice if we got out of here?" Riley whispers in my ear, her voice seductive and low, and I shiver from head to toe.

I reach over and tap Andrea on the shoulder. "Not one word from you..." I warn her. "We're out of here. We'll see you in the morning."

Andrea only smirks and nods.

We leave the room before the comedian can target us, and Riley reaches for my hand, intertwining our fingers. I look down at our hands and then back up at her, my face breaking into a smile.

The energy is palpable as we walk to the cabin, sharing looks and trying to keep our hands to ourselves.

We make it to the cabin, and as soon as the door closes, I'm shoved up against it. My senses are flooded with the saltwater lingering on her skin and the perfume used to cover it up.

"Fucking finally," Riley is already nipping at my throat, her hands going to the bottom of my shirt. My skin tingles everywhere she touches.

"Shouldn't we talk about this?" I gasp as my shirt is ripped over my head, and Riley attaches herself to my lips.

"Later," she twirls her tongue around mine and drops to her knees, kissing down, making me whimper.

My hands go to her hair as she places open-mouth kisses on my stomach. "Rye, bed." I manage to choke out as I pull her back to her feet.

Our lips collide as I walk her backwards to the bed, stripping her shirt off and unhooking her bra, throwing them behind me. Her knees hit the edge of the bed, and I push her down, standing over her.

"Fuck," I groan as I drink her in, half-naked and sprawled out before me.

She is the most breathtaking person I have ever seen.

She smirks and props herself up, making her bare breasts look even more exquisite.

"I love you, Lex. But if you don't fuck me in the next minute, I'll handle it myself."

I can't decide if that's a threat or a promise, but who am I to keep her waiting?

I unhook my bra and strip out of my pants before bending down to unbutton Riley's shorts. I slowly trail the zipper down, earning myself a glare, but it's worth it. Grasping the hem of her shorts, I pull them off her legs, followed by her underwear. I can smell her arousal, and it makes me dizzy with want.

She's bare before me, eyes alight and body on display, and I can't help but stare in reverence.

"You are..." I take a deep breath. "So fucking beautiful."

Riley sits up with a blush and kisses me, pushing my underwear off my hips and grabbing me by the back of the neck to pull me on top of her.

The moment my bare skin touches hers, I've never been more sure of anything.

CHAPTER TEN

She just needed a moment of solitude.

A moment to breathe and to think about her life and where it was headed.

A moment away from everyone to just feel.

Reaching the uppermost deck, she spotted an open clamshell lounger and headed toward it, content to relax while contemplating her future. One other couple was sunbathing, but they were quiet and did nothing to interrupt the peace she was searching for. The upper deck was barren since most people had gone on excursions or to the city to explore the local shops at the port.

She got comfortable and watched the ocean spread out before her. She stared into the vast waters that spanned for miles and miles on every side. It was then that she realized just how meager humans were compared to nature.

Where do I go from here? How does life change so drastically in an instant?

"Excuse me," someone bent down to peek into the lounger. "Would you like a drink from the bar?"

She smiled kindly at them. "No, thank you. I'm fine."

The bartender nodded. "We're at the bottom of the stairs if you change your mind."

He went to the other couple on the deck, and they also declined, stating that they were just about to leave. Once the bartender retreated to the bar, the couple gathered their things and followed him to the lower decks.

Solitude. True solitude.

The woman closed her eyes around the tears threatening to fall, one escaping, making its way down her cheek. She brushed it away angrily, not wanting to break down during this cruise. She could do that later, once she was home.

She breathed in the salty air and enjoyed the quiet.

Thinking. Planning.

"Are you okay?" Another voice asked from outside the lounger, casting a shadow over her.

A shaky breath, wishing to be left alone. "Yes, thank you."

"Didn't feel like being with everyone else?"

Her skin prickled. The tone of voice had shifted into something strange, detached.

Into something cold.

They appeared over the lounger's roof to look at her.

"I'm just trying to enjoy the peace and quiet for a little," she explained.

"That's understandable." They smiled, but it didn't reach their eyes. "I always welcome the quiet... until it gets maddeningly unbearable."

Suddenly, there's a blinding glint of sunlight, and it throws her off briefly before she can comprehend what is happening.

By the time her mind catches up that there is danger, it's already too late.

They had already jumped into the lounger and straddled her, pinning her down with their weight while she struggled underneath them.

They're relentless, unmoving, and she couldn't break free.

"Get off of me!" She screamed and thrashed. "What the fuck is wrong with you?"

They smiled, big and happy. "Go ahead and scream. No one can hear you."

They were right - the activities on the ship were too loud to be heard up on this deck.

She fought with everything in her, but the person on top of her was at an advantage. They managed to pin her arms under their knees, leaving no room for her to break free.

The scalpel, sharp in their hand, looked menacing as they stared her in the eyes before looking at her arm.

"No, please." Sobbing, her mind racing with how to free herself and coming up empty.

The person reached down to one of her arms and placed the sharp scalpel gently into the crook of her elbow. They applied pressure as they dragged the sharp edge down to her wrist.

"Such a shame. They'll all think you couldn't bear this life anymore," they tsk menacingly before moving to her other arm.

She could feel the cold metal on her skin, but more than that, she could feel the life beginning to drain from her.

The beat from the music on the main deck pounded in her ears, and her mind began to go fuzzy.

"Please don't." She said softly, losing her strength. "Please stop."

The person ignored her as they moved to her other arm and released her.

They left the shade of the lounger to stand before it, watching as she struggled to stop the bleeding.

The blood pools beneath her as she sobs.

She's lightheaded. The sun dims in her line of sight as the darkness closes in.

Her heartbeats slow, and she knows she's dying.

She had no strength left to move, but she looked at them with glassy eyes.

"Fuck you." She spat; her voice lost in the wind.

Our lives were just starting.

So many dreams for us.

Gone.

Chapter Eleven

I'm woken by kisses on my bare shoulder and hands roaming my body under the soft sheets. I keep my eyes closed, reveling in the moment, before I turn around to look at the seductress before me.

"Good morning," Riley smirks, bending down to take a nipple in her mouth from where the sheets have fallen, leaving my skin exposed.

"Indeed, it is." I groan, running my fingers through her hair.

She releases my nipple with a playful nip of her teeth before making her way up my neck to my mouth. She places a soft, deep kiss on my lips, and I drown in her.

We break the kiss with a deep breath.

"Can we just lie around here all day?" I wonder. "Do you think we'll be missed?"

Riley moves so that she is lying on top of me, and she props herself up on her fists on my breastbone. "I think we might get a few questions if we do that."

I raise an eyebrow. "So, we're talking about this now?"

Riley smiles. "Well, apparently we have really great sex, so I'm not sure what there is to discuss."

I roll my eyes. "You told me you loved me."

Riley kisses my bare skin again and smirks. "Yep."

"I haven't told you that I love you yet."

She leans up to kiss my lips. "You just did," she whispers with a breathtaking smile.

"So, it's just... that easy?"

"It is." She nods. "But now I'd like to call you my girlfriend instead of my best friend."

"How about both?" I grin and grab her face, kissing her hard. "And how do you feel about telling everyone?"

"Babe," She chuckles. "I'd go to the ends of the earth for you. I have no problem with everyone knowing."

My face breaks out into the biggest smile, and I nod. "I feel the same way," I whisper and kiss her again, gently and lovingly.

I can't believe that this is real.

***

Thanks to our morning in bed, Riley and I are late for brunch, so we send a quick message to the group while rushing to get ready. We dance around each other in the small cabin, trying to brush our teeth and get dressed, and laugh as we keep bumping into one another.

We finally make it to brunch, and Andrea and Pru are smirking at us as the rest of the group converses.

"Good morning, you two." Dre arches an eyebrow at us. Riley and I share a look and roll our eyes in sync. "You going to get the French Toast again after your workout, Rye?" she teases.

We sit beside each other in the two open chairs, and Riley looks Andrea dead in the eye. "That's a great idea. I'm famished."

Andrea feigns a gag, but the smile on her lips gives her away.

"What did I miss?" Sean asks, looking between all of us. "Why do I feel like I missed something?"

Andrea pats him on the knee. "Don't worry about it, baby."

Plans for the day are discussed over drinks while we wait for the food. Hannah, Claire, and Pru have booked massages in the spa. Sean and George want to get off the ship and shop, and we are content to follow wherever. Once the massages and shopping are over, we decide to meet for Bingo before dinner.

Our food comes out hot and perfect, and we dive into the fluffy eggs, French Toast, pancakes, and bacon set on the table. Everyone shares bites of their plates.

"You want a bite?" Riley says around a mouthful of her French Toast. "It's amazing."

I nod and reach over with my fork to stab a piece. I grin as I bring the dripping piece to my mouth.

"You got a little..." Riley points to the side of her mouth, but then pauses and gives me a wicked smile.

"Rye," I warn her with narrowed eyes.

She leans over and licks the corner of my mouth where syrup has dripped. Her tongue is warm and wet, and then it is in my mouth, and we're kissing like it's the most normal thing in the world.

"Excuse me, but what the fuck is happening?" Claire's voice breaks through, and we separate.

Everyone is practically gawking at us except Andrea and Pru, who are both grinning ear to ear. George looks on in surprised amusement, Sean has his mouth dropped open, and the other girls stare at us in shock.

"Yeah, so..." I laugh. "Rye and I are together."

Everyone sighs and starts talking to each other, ignoring us.

"How much do I owe? Who won?" Hannah pouts and crosses her arms across her chest.

"I did!" George exclaims, shooting a thumbs up at me and Riley.

"Are you sure? I think I won." Pru declares. "I said the middle of the cruise. You had the beginning." She narrows her eyes at George.

Sean shakes his head. "I think it's a tie." He tilts his head in contemplation.

"You were betting on us?" My jaw drops.

Andrea shrugs. "You two were the only dumbasses who didn't realize. We've been waiting for months."

Riley squints her eyes and then grabs my hand. "It would have been nice if someone had told us," she whines.

"We did!" Everyone yells simultaneously, turning heads from the tables next to us.

***

Once brunch is finished, we separate with a promise to meet up for Bingo at four. That gives us five hours to entertain ourselves before reconvening. Hannah, Claire, and Pru head to their massages, and everyone else decides to stay on the boat instead of dealing with the hassle of checkpoints getting on and off the ship.

The Lido Deck is having a party, so we grab some fresh drinks and strip down to our bathing suits. Sean and George have decided to join an arm-wrestling contest, so we hang out on the lounge chairs until it starts.

"I'm already out of my drink." Riley sighs heavily, like it's the worst thing ever. "Does anyone need another?"

She stands up and stretches, and I look at all the skin on display and feel that heat pool low in my stomach again.

"Lexi, please keep the eye fucking to a minimum, okay?" George chides as he watches me check Riley out.

"Absolutely not," I say immediately.

Riley smirks and goes to get a new round of drinks. She's standing at the bar when James approaches, and I immediately feel jealousy rearing up in my chest.

"Better go get your girl!" Andrea prods me when James reaches out to touch Riley's arm.

I scramble to get up and try not to run over to them, and I come up behind Riley and wrap my arms around her waist. "James." I acknowledge the man coldly.

Riley chuckles and squeezes my arms around her as she leans back into me. "Hi, baby."

James' eyebrows shoot up into his hairline, and then he smiles. "I see you finally told her then?"

Riley returns the smile and nods. "Figured it was time."

James looks at me and nods, the defeat evident on his face. "You're a lucky woman, Lexi." He then turns around and walks away.

"What the hell just happened?" I wonder, and Riley throws her head back onto my shoulder and laughs.

"I had no idea you were so jealous." Riley spins in my arms and wraps her arms around my neck.

"I didn't either," I admit. "I saw him over here with you and almost lost it. I'm sorry."

She briefly kisses my lips. "Don't be. It's hot," she smirks.

"Oh yeah?" I grin and tighten my hold around her before I let her go to help carry the drinks.

We return to the group and sit for a while, sunbathing and having an easy conversation. The sun is shining bright in the afternoon sky, and the music is loud but not obnoxiously so, pumping out a hip-hop beat that people nod to.

We're in the middle of people watching when a loud shout suddenly comes behind us.

"No man, fuck you!"

I duck as something flies past my head, and I spin around angrily to see what the fuck is going on.

Two teenage boys have gotten into a fight and are squaring up to each other. They're standing there, glaring at each other. The next thing we know, they are throwing punches instead of throwing things at each other. A terrified teenage girl stands there begging them to stop fighting. Chairs are flying as they are shoved out of the way because of the fight.

"Jesus Christ," George mutters before he and Sean hop out of their seats and try to break up the fight.

The teens have each other in headlocks when the guys get there and try to pry them apart. Sean slips in on the taller kid's left, prying at the elbow. George hooks the other around the waist and drags him two steps back.

This time, the girl yells at Sean and George, telling them to leave them alone. Riley, Dre, and I all sigh and stand up to help.

"You're going to get kicked off the ship if you don't stop, " Sean tells one of the boys firmly as he tries to get him to let go of the other boy.

George slips to the right to avoid a flying fist and yanks on the kid in his arms. "Oh hell no."

"They just started fighting for no reason!" The girl cries as we reach her.

"Yeah, like that's believable," Andrea mutters.

Sean and George separate the kids by grabbing them around the waist and physically pulling them apart when security makes it onto the deck and heads our way. It's Keith, Theodore, and another officer.

"Everyone, take a step back from each other!" Keith booms. "All four of you, back up and put your hands up."

Sean goes wide-eyed and obeys. "We were just trying to get them to stop fighting!"

"Yo, man, we aren't part of this," George adds, putting his hands into the air.

The teens prove their point when they go for each other again.

Theodore rolls his eyes and motions for George and Sean to back away as they go to the kids. Keith and the other officer drag them apart, leading them to opposite deck sides.   Theodore turns to all of us and squints at me and Riley. "You two."

I give him a grimace. "Hello." I point to the young girl. "She's the one who will probably have your answers."

"Seems like trouble likes to follow you lot." Theodore looks at all of us with a crooked grin.

Riley frowns. "We were just trying to relax, and they started fighting behind us. We had nothing to do with it."

Theodore smiles. "We're going to have to keep our eyes on you guys, " he jokes, and we all half-heartedly laugh as he takes the girl aside to speak to her.

After our relaxing afternoon is interrupted, we attempt to get back into chill mode before meeting with the rest of the group. It only takes two more drinks, and then we're on the deck dancing like nothing happened.

***

Pru and Claire find us before four, drunk on the Lido deck and laughing at Sean and George in the arm-wrestling contest.

"How were your massages?" Riley's words are slightly slurred.

"Amazing," Claire sighs dreamily. "It was just what I needed."

Pru sips her beer. "Much needed," she agrees. "Hannah decided to go back to her room and nap before dinner."

Claire perks up. "Hey, why don't we look for clues for the game while there aren't so many people on the ship instead of Bingo?"

I frown and reach for Riley's hand, drunkenly missing at first and having to try again. "I don't wanna." I tilt my head in defiance.

Pru rolls her eyes. "How about I stick with Claire and help her? Rye can go with you and help with our clues. That way, you don't have to be separated for more than 5 minutes."

A lazy smile crosses my lips. "That's a good idea."

Claire's smile grows as she bounces up and down and looks at Pru. "Let's divide and conquer, babe. I have some ideas!"

We told Andrea about the plan, and she decided to stay on the deck, hang out with the guys, and have a few more drinks.

Riley and I finish the rest of our drinks before telling Andrea we will see them all in a little while.

Riley attaches herself to me, and she squeezes my hand. "I need to go get something out of the room," she wiggles her eyebrows at me.

We rush to the room, not paying attention to anything around us. We reach our cabin door, barely registering the piece of paper in our bin outside the door, and grab it quickly before we are on each other as soon as it slams shut behind us.

***

I roll off Riley and lie on my back, panting with a smile. "I don't think I'll ever get tired of that."

Riley breathes heavily and rolls over to face me, drawing patterns on my bare skin. "Thank God."

We lie together peacefully before I remember the paper outside our door. I place a kiss on her lips before I hop out of bed and grab it off the dresser. Opening it up, I frown.

It's time to relax and unwind,

On the quietest deck you will find,

Something special that is one of a kind.

"What is it?" Riley sits up to look at me, a questioning look on her face.

"It's a clue."

"Do they personally leave clues?"

I shrug. "Maybe it's because Pru and I have only found one? We signed up for additional help and extra clues."

"Have you two even tried at all?" She laughs.

I shake my head. "Nope!" I read the clue out loud. "I guess we should get dressed and try to figure this out before meeting everyone." I look at the clock. "We have an hour and a half."   Riley stands, the sheets falling away from her, and I can't help but leer. "Or we could stay here."

Riley laughs with a shake of her head. "You're insatiable. Let's find this clue and continue this later."

***

We get dressed and wander for about 30 minutes before Riley proclaims it might be the adult-only area at the ship's topmost deck. We arrive there to find the group of doctors from the first day.

They are all yelling, not at each other, but at everyone who has started gathering around.

"Get back! You need to stay away from here." One of the men says sternly to a younger couple trying to get around him.

There's a rope tied across the stairs with a sign that says, "Closed for Cleaning." That doesn't explain why these men are so adamant about people not going up the stairs; most people are probably trying to find a quiet spot and don't care about the sign.

Riley and I look at each other in dread at the commotion, and my heart starts to pound in my ears. We rush up to the man and try to push past him.

"No one can go back there," he says, arms held out to block us.

"Let me through," I growl, low and threatening.

"I can't do that, " he sighs. We have to wait for security."

I don't need to look at Riley this time before we shove past him and rush around the corner.

And there he is.

James.

Covered in blood. Dark and red.

Everywhere.

CHAPTER TWELVE

"Please, don't come closer," James begs, bloody hands shaking as he kneels next to a clamshell lounger. "You don't need... Not like this."

Ice floods my veins.

Ignoring his desperate plea, we rush forward, our steps pounding in the silence.

Hannah is inside.

Pale. Unmoving.

Dead.

Her arms are slit open from elbow to wrist.

The blood pools around the lounger from the sheer amount of it.

Riley lets out a cry of anguish and skitters back, falling to her knees, hands over her mouth.

A metallic smell hangs in the air, and the sight of it everywhere is overwhelming.

I stare in shock, rooted to my spot, my legs threatening to give out from under me.

As James stands up, something breaks in me.

"You fucking bastard!" I run to him and push him hard in the chest.

"Lexi, wait!" James holds his bloody hands up as my fists weakly rain down on him. "We... we came up, and she was already like this! I tried to help, Lexi! I did CPR, but she wouldn't wake up!" He grabs my flying hands and grips them tightly. "Security is on its way."

His voice is firm yet gentle, and I shatter.

Riley is sobbing behind me, and I wrestle free from James to go to her. I drop to the floor beside her, my arms shaking as I pull her to me. The tears come in an unrelenting wave, my chest tightening with every sob she lets out.

This can't be happening. Not to *her*.

Oh Hannah.

She's always the one to laugh at my stupid jokes. She's always so kind.

Was... she *was* always so kind.

"I want to go home," Riley gasps through her tears. "I want everything to go back to normal."

I kiss her head and hold her tight while we wait for security.

Keith and Theodore show up moments later and ignore us as they make a beeline for Hannah.

"Oh, fucking hell." Theodore groans, puts a hand to his mouth, and turns away. Keith hangs his head, and I can see the heavy sigh from where I sit.

Theodore barks into his radio, his voice cracking. "Brightstar! We need medical now."

They talk to James, spit-firing a million questions about what happened and what he knows, before Theodore notices us. His face drops, and he walks over to us, crouching to get eye level.

His voice is strained, a quiet command, but even he seems shaken. "Let's get you both out of here... now."

I go to protest, not wanting to move, but Riley nods, and I stand with her, allowing the officer to guide us away.

Away from Hannah.

Away from our friend.

I look behind me one last time before we leave the deck, only seeing legs sticking out from the lounger, and I choke back a whimper.

I don't want to leave her like this. Alone. Surrounded by strangers.

I stop walking, about to turn around, when Theodore stops me. "There's nothing you can do. You can't stay here." I can see the anguish in his eyes and lose all the fight in me.

I relent and nod my head, following Riley down the stairs.

***

Numb, hollowed out, we follow Theodore as he guides us back to our room. The ocean air that once felt fresh now churns in my chest, tainted by the scent of sunscreen and salty tears that refuse to stop falling.

As we reach our cabin, Theodore promises to check in on us later.

Riley and I enter the room and go to the bed, sitting on the edge side by side.

There are no words to say.

Riley finally looks at me as I stare at my hands, noticing the blood on them from when James grabbed me. I try to rub it off to no avail.

Riley hiccups, the sound almost like she's choking on her own heartache, and she looks at me through a blur of tears. "Oh my God, Hannah. How did this happen?" Her shoulders heave with her sobs.

I stare at the wall.

After a moment, Riley looks up with a pained expression. "Lex, we have to tell them." She sniffles. "Jesus Christ. How are we going to tell them?"

I close my eyes and shake my head. "I don't know if I can. I don't think I can."

Riley reaches for my hand, and I yank it back, still staring at the blood.

Hannah's blood.

Riley sighs and wipes her eyes, standing up to pace. "It would be better for us to tell them than the crew."

She's right. Fuck, she's right.

I've never wanted to curl up and ignore the world as much as I do right now.

"Where should we message them to meet us?" I wipe my eye on my shoulder.

"Here?" Riley suggests, placing her hand on my arm. "I'll message them while you clean up."

I nod and stand shakily, mindlessly going to the bathroom and turning on the water.

I scrub my arms until they are raw. The soap has washed away the blood, but still I scrub.

I can still see it on my hands, even though the water is running clear and nothing is there; my mind is playing tricks on me.

***

Ten minutes later, a pounding at our door makes both of us jump. After washing my hands, I joined Riley on the bed to wait for the others.

We share a look, and I lean over and place a kiss on Riley's lips. "I love you." I rasp out.

"I love you, too," Riley whispers. She takes a deep breath and gets off the bed. With a resigned sigh, she opens the door. "Hey, guys. Come in."

The group files in and finds a spot in the small cabin. They stare at us with mixed expressions.

"George..." Riley starts, and then the tears form. She opens her mouth to say something, but closes it with a shake of her head as she turns around to face me.

"What the fuck is going on?" Pru asks, her usually calm voice raised and anxious, feeding off our energy.

I look to Riley, and she breaks eye contact, looking down at the floor. Her tears are already flowing. I take a deep breath.

"George. Sit down." I say softly

George doesn't move. "Where is Hannah?" He demands and looks around. "Why isn't she here?"

I choke back a sob, take a deep breath, and brace myself. "George, I am so sorry..."

George goes pale. "Where is she? Is she hurt?"

"Riley and I found Hannah on the upper deck." I start crying, unable to hold it back any longer. "She's dead."

George's knees give out, and he has to catch himself on the wall as he stares at us. He keeps repeating "no" over and over and begins to dry heave.

Riley comes and holds my hand. Andrea gasps. Sean runs a hand through his hair and shakes his head. Pru and Claire both hold back their tears.

"What?" George wails in anguish. "What do you mean she's dead?"

"Her wrists were slit," Riley explains quietly.

Everyone cries out and starts talking at the same time.

"How do you even know this?" Claire stares at us suspiciously.

"Why the fuck was she up there?" Pru asks.

Andrea's fists clench at her sides. "Are you even sure it's Hannah?"

"No." George shakes his head. "No, you're lying. Hannah wouldn't do that." He sits on the couch and puts his head in his hands. "I don't know what kind of sick joke you're playing, but it's not fucking funny. She messaged me 30 minutes ago saying she would meet us for dinner."

Sean goes to George and sits beside him, putting a hand on his shoulder.

"I wish I were joking," I say. "We couldn't let you find out from someone else."

"Hannah wouldn't kill herself!" George explodes. "She wouldn't." He stares at each of us before his shoulders hunch. "She's pregnant," he whispers.

Sean sits up straight on the couch and stares at George, shocked. Andrea cries by the doorway, holding herself. Pru and Clair are wrapped in a tight hug as they cry. I feel Riley stiffen next to me.

"We found out right before we left. We were planning on telling everyone on the last night." George stares blankly ahead. "She wouldn't kill herself." His voice is firm.

A knock on the door startles us all. I hop up to answer it and find Keith and Theodore standing on the other side.

"Lexi," Keith looks past me into the room. "We need to talk to you—to all of you. Why don't you guys come with us?"

"It's just for some information," Theodore explains. "No one is in trouble," he clarifies.

George comes to the doorway. "It's true? Hannah is dead?"

Theodore frowns and slowly nods. "Are you George Cooper?"

George stands up straighter. "I am."

Keith looks around the hallway where people are coming back to the ship. "Let's go talk somewhere away from everyone."

***

"Lexi," Theodore says as he and Keith enter the room I've been put in.

I gulp. "That's me," I try to joke, but it falls flat.

"What can you tell me about today?" Keith sighs as he sits down across from me. Theodore continues to stand near the door.

I look between them. "Uhh... well, we had brunch and then split up for a little. Riley and I were looking for clues for the murder-mystery game, and our clue led us to the top deck."

My mind immediately replays finding Hannah.

How lifeless she was.

How dark the blood was.

The officers both look at me with sympathy.

"Your group seems surrounded by bad luck," Keith says softly. "Was there any indication that Hannah was planning this?"

I can't get what George said out of my head - Hannah was pregnant. My brain is processing what George said earlier about how Hannah wouldn't do this.

I speak slowly. "Everyone assumes she killed herself. What if she didn't?"

The men share a look. "It's pretty clear that the wounds were self-inflicted," Theodore says gently. "We found a scalpel next to her."

"Theo," Keith warns with a shake of his head.

I narrow my eyes at the two of them. "You call us bad luck, but why *always* you two? Every damn time something goes wrong, you two are always the ones that show up."

"Because we're security on this boat," Keith says, matter-of-factly. "Would you expect someone else?"

I stand up. "No, I expect security. But are you two the only ones on this whole boat?" I start to pace, my mind racing.

"There are sixteen of us. Four watch the cameras, four are supervisors, including Keith. The rest of us are split by deck. Keith and I stick together for our rounds on the assigned decks." Theodore explains.

My mouth turns downward. "And we just so happen to keep running into you when shit hits the fan?"

Suspicion clouds everything.

"Lexi, we are just trying to figure out what happened today." Keith leans back in his chair.   "Please. Was there anything at all that would make Hannah want to hurt herself?"

I whirl around to gape at the men. "James."

Theodore raises a brow. "James?"

"James," I spit out, the anger making me shake. "He keeps popping up everywhere. And he found her. He was there when we..." I shake my head, unable to finish my thought. "You have to talk to him. He did something to her." I cough, my throat dry.

"Let me grab you some water." Theodore leaves the room, leaving Keith and me alone.

"Lexi, we talked to James."

"Talk to him again!" I yell, my eyes flooding with tears. "He was there. He was there, and she's dead. That can't be just a coincidence."

Keith says nothing at my outburst, and I take a deep breath and sit back down. "Did George tell you that she was pregnant?" The tears start to fall.

She'll never meet her baby. She'll never be a mother. She'll never hold that precious life and watch them grow up.

She'll never do anything ever again.

"I am very sorry about your friend," Keith says, resigned. "Let me take you back to the others."

"Will you please look further into James. I know she didn't kill herself, Keith. She wouldn't have," my voice is determined and strong, even through my tears.

"We're going to explore every angle, I promise you." Keith's jaw tightens, and I want to believe him.

His words are supposed to be comforting, but I can't find the strength to believe them.

I can't believe anything anymore.

CHAPTER THIRTEEN

By the time Keith leads me back to the main deck, the rest of the group is gone, and I am alone. I pull out my phone to see messages from everyone.

Where is everyone? - Sean

They just let me go. Meet me in the Atrium. - Andrea

Guys... I can't believe this is real. - Claire

We're coming to you. Stay there. - Pru

George? - Sean

I need to be alone. Just... leave me alone. - George

Lexi? Where the fuck are you? - Riley

I'm on my way. - Me

Rounding the corner into the Atrium, I'm immediately swallowed in a desperate hug. Riley clings to me like she's afraid I'll vanish, nuzzling her face into my neck. I grip her back just as tightly.

Over her shoulder, I find the others.

Shell-shocked. Empty.

"Should we check on George?" I ask, my voice cracked.

Sean shakes his head. "If it were me," he gulps, "I'd want a moment to myself. I know him. He'll come to us when he's ready." He hangs his head, and Andrea puts her arm around his waist.

"What do we do now?" Claire whispers. "What happens next?" She hugs herself.

"I have no idea," I admit. Riley finally pulls back, but her hand stays laced with mine.

Sean looks at his watch. "It's seven. We should probably eat something."

Claire flinches. "I don't think I can eat. I can't sit there with everyone and act like nothing happened."

Pru lets out a long breath. "Sean is right. We need to eat something. Let's go to the buffet instead of sitting in the dining room."

My eyes are unfocused as I follow the group. Riley is tucked under my arm, and I can feel her shaking.

We silently grab plates and get dinner, sitting at one of the tables away from everyone else.

I stare at the food in front of me, unable to eat. I push the food around on my plate.

My leg shakes anxiously beneath the table, and my mind is racing.

"I don't think she did it," I murmur, barely above a whisper.

Andrea recoils like she's been slapped. "What? What did they tell you?"

I shake my head. "They didn't tell me anything. I just... know."

"Lex—" Riley starts, squeezing my hand gently, but I'm past the point of caution.

"Three deaths and a missing couple on one cruise. You seriously think that's normal?" My voice rises. "This isn't random. Someone is doing this."

Pru's fork clatters to her plate. "You sound insane."

"I'm not," I snap, my breath shallow. I force myself to calm down, taking a deep breath. "Someone is doing this. It's not random."

Pru abruptly stands, her chair scraping against the floor. "I can't listen to this." She spits out and storms away.

Claire blinks through tears, whispering, "I'm sorry," before hurrying after Pru.

Andrea exchanges a glance with Sean, then looks at me, hesitantly.

"I'll figure it out," I say before she can open her mouth.

Riley's fingers thread tightly through mine.

"I believe you," she says quietly. "I'm with you."

For the first time tonight, I don't feel like I'm drowning alone.

***

After dinner, Riley and I retreat to our room. We open the cabin door, flip on the light, and pause in the doorway as the air carries the ghost of George's sobs.

A tear slips down my cheek, and I feel Riley brush it away with trembling fingers.

"What do you need?" she asks gently.

I close my eyes and shake my head. "Right now, I just want to sleep. I want to sleep and pretend none of this happened."

"Okay," the corner of her lip quirks up in a forced smile, and she leads me toward the bed.

She gently grabs the bottom of my shirt and looks me in the eye. I nod, and she slowly strips the shirt from me. She takes off my bra and places a gentle kiss on my neck. She finishes taking off my clothes, helps me put on a T-shirt to sleep, and guides me into bed. She pulls the covers up over me and places the softest of kisses on my lips.

"I'm with you," she repeats from earlier. "I love you."

"Thank you," I whisper and pull her into another kiss. "I love you."

She smiles as she stands up and grabs her book off the bedside table. "I don't think I can sleep right now. I'll be right out on the balcony reading if you need me, okay?" Her voice shakes, and I know she wants to fall apart alone for a while.

"Okay," I nod and close my eyes, hoping to fall into a dreamless sleep.

***

I wake up with a gasp, heart jackhammering out of my chest, and my shirt damp with sweat. It's dark around me, and I can feel the ship sway from side to side as we travel.

I sit up, run a hand through my sweaty hair, and look around. The light for the balcony is still on, and Riley isn't in bed next to me.

I swing my legs over the side of the bed and pad my way to the balcony door. I open it to find Rye sitting there, the book closed, staring into the dark ocean. I can tell her mind is racing. My lips turn down in a frown, and I sit in the empty chair beside her.

"Couldn't sleep?" I wonder, and she shakes her head. "I had a dream it was you," I swallow thickly.

Riley turns away from the water to look at me. She stands up and comes to my chair, sitting on my lap and wrapping herself around me. "I'm right here." She shivers, and I know it's not only from the night air.

We sit silently, listening to the ship cut through the water and looking out at the stars. Finally, chilled and exhausted, we go inside, crawl into bed, and hold each other through the rest of the night.

***

The next morning, a knock jolts me awake. I groan as Riley pushes me out of bed to answer it.

Pru stands there, fully dressed and wired tight.

"What the hell are you doing?" I yawn.

"Zip lining," she says flatly. "We all are. Get dressed."

I gape at her. "Pru, there's no way-"

Pru brushes past me into the room, and Riley sits up, stunned. "We are stuck on this ship until Saturday. We have two more days, and I won't sit around and fucking lose my mind over everything. Now get up," she directs at Riley, "and both of you get dressed." She says firmly.

Claire appears in the doorway, pale with bags under her eyes, and shrugs helplessly. "She won't give up."

I know that people react differently to death, but I didn't expect Pru to hop out of bed and decide that an excursion would be the solution. We haven't seen George since yesterday and have no idea how he is or what he wants.

Riley and I catch each other's eye and nod. She gets out of bed and puts a hand on Pru's shoulder. "Okay," she says. "We'll go zip-lining. Give us ten minutes."

Pru wordlessly nods and leaves the cabin.

Claire sighs. "She's determined to forget about yesterday."

"We'll meet you guys in the Atrium. Did you get in touch with anyone else?" I wonder, forcing myself to act like this is just another day, and one of our friends isn't dead.

This is so wrong.

"She's been to everyone's cabins. Including George's," she winces.

Riley sighs deeply. "How is he?"

Claire's eyes cloud over with tears. "Barely holding it together. Maybe... maybe don't be all coupley today around him."

"He's coming with us?" Riley gawks as Claire nods.

"Got it," I say. "We'll meet you guys there."

Once they're gone, Riley and I get ready in heavy silence.

***

Once we're dressed, we meet everyone, and I scan their faces. Pru's face is pinched tight, and Claire keeps nervously looking at her. Andrea and Sean are leaning on each other, exhausted. Riley is wringing her hands nervously and looking at George, who looks like he aged 10 years overnight.

"Please stop looking at me like that," George begs, his voice rough, aimed at Riley.

Everyone holds their breath for a moment.

"I'm sorry," she whispers, eyes dropping. "Are you sure you're up for this?"

It's the question that I know everyone is thinking but was too afraid to ask.

"No," George says. "I'm not 'up' for any of this. But I can't sit in my room, our room, and stare at the wall. I can't stay there without her." He looks a million miles away, and my heart breaks for him.

Riley hesitantly walks up to him and wraps him in a hug. "Whatever you need, you let us know," she says quietly.

"We need to go," Pru says, checking her watch.

Andrea whirls on her, fury on her face. "Goddammit, Pru. No one fucking cares about zip-lining right now!"

Pru looks around the group, her face scrunched up before it crumples. She swipes angrily at her eyes.

We all fall silent and stare at each other. The Atrium bustles around us, music playing and people milling around, but none of that matters in this moment.

Pru's tears fall, and George walks up to her and cradles her cheek. "Come on. Let's go." He jerks his head and starts leading the way.

We all follow, broken, pretending that this is another day where our friend isn't dead.

CHAPTER FOURTEEN

Heart hammering in chest, the teen looked around behind him, double-checking no one was watching, as he slipped into the stairwell.

His friends had dared him to sneak into the galley and steal a live lobster. He knew he could get caught, maybe even kicked off the ship after the fight he was involved in earlier, but the idea of impressing the girl he had met on the first night shoved the second thoughts out of his mind.

He crept down the hallway, pressing himself flat against the wall as he tried to navigate through the darkness.

The corridor's doors loomed, threatening to burst open at any second. He shivered, ignoring the screaming warnings now flashing in his head.

A door slammed somewhere behind him.

He dropped into a crouch, making himself smaller as voices floated down the hall.

His heart pounded so hard he thought it might explode. The voices grew louder, closer, and he squeezed his eyes shut, praying he wouldn't piss himself.

Footsteps thudded on the stairwell above, followed by the creak of the deck door. He held his breath until the footsteps faded into the distance.

Letting out a shaky sigh, he stood up and shook himself off.

"You got this," he whispered, forcing himself to keep moving.

Tunnel-visioned as he focused on his goal, he didn't hear the person come up behind him until it was too late.

"You shouldn't be here," a voice growled in his ear, low and menacing.

A hand clamped over his mouth, cutting off his scream before it could start. An arm locked around his throat, crushing his air supply. He thrashed wildly, but the grip tightened, stronger than anything he could fight. Black spots bloomed behind his eyes. His body sagged, tears slipping free.

"You really fucked up, kid," the voice snarled in his ear, breath rank against his cheek.

The hand over his mouth vanished. Before he could even gasp, two hands gripped the sides of his head and wrenched.

A loud crack resounded in the empty hallway.

Images burst behind his eyes: the girl he'd liked, his friends laughing, the bright sun on the beach they'd spent the day on.

Pain.

Finality.

"Mommy" he thought, but the word never left his lips.

CHAPTER FIFTEEN

The hole that Hannah has left in our group is felt from the moment we step off the boat. Our typical banter has been replaced with silence, and the tension in the air is thicker than the humidity outside. No one is looking at each other, and I can sense that none of us really wants to be doing this.

We quietly march to the bus that will take us to our excursion, where Sean sits next to George so he isn't alone. Riley and I squeeze into a seat with Andrea, even though Riley must sit on my lap.

"How are you?" I ask my sister as she has her head down, dejected.

"How do you think?" She scoffs, making me sigh.

The bus driver approaches us with a scowl and looks at Riley. "You need to find an actual seat."

"Fuck off." Riley snaps, shoving her way onto the bench next to us.

The man already sitting on the seat stares at her, horrified, as she moves him out of the way, elbowing him until he is pressed into the bus's wall.

Andrea stares blankly out the window. Behind us, Pru and Claire trade sharp whispers.

The ride is miserable.

When the bus finally stops, we gather at the edge of the excursion group and trail behind toward the ziplining course.

No one's listening to the guide's instructions, and I wonder, fleetingly, if this is a good idea. It's not like zip-lining without knowing what we're doing is safe.

As we gear up for the lines, Pru stands alone, trying to buckle one of her leg straps while the attendants are all busy helping other people. She fumbles with the strap, her hands jerky, and her face flushed an ugly red. I hesitate, then walk over and swat her hand away, buckling the damn thing myself.

I straighten up. Pru stares past me, forehead slick with sweat, brow knotted tight.

"Thanks," she mumbles.

"You good?" I ask and immediately regret it.

Her eyes snap to mine, and she glares at me. "How can you even ask that?"

I wince. "Sorry. You're right."

Pru puts her helmet on and yanks the chin strap tight. "Hannah is dead. And you're acting insane, Lexi. No, I am not fucking good."

She brushes past me, her shoulder hitting mine harder than accidentally, and I stand alone.

***

At the halfway point, we stopped at a hut where lunch was served to everyone. We were sweaty and tired, but everyone's mood had temporarily lifted.

Zipping through the trees like you're flying will do that, I guess.

Riley and I are seated at a table with Claire, who looks like she's about to jump out of her skin. She darts glances over her shoulder before snapping her gaze back to us. Her eyes skitter back and forth between us. Her knee bounces against the table, and her hands won't stay still as she rips the napkin in them apart.

And then she drops a bomb.

"Pru proposed last night," she blurts.

Riley gasps.

My mouth falls open. "What?" I yell.

"Shh!" Claire waves a frantic hand at us, her eyes wild. "She's losing it, guys. Like... actually losing it. She discussed how we can look at rings when we get home and start planning."

"What did you say?" Riley leans in, dropping her voice to a whisper.

"I told her I didn't think right now was the best time to make these decisions," Claire mumbles into her hands, then drags them down her face. "What else was I supposed to say? She was going on about how she couldn't lose anyone else."

"So, marriage is the answer?" Riley scoffs.

I glance over Claire's shoulder at the rest of the group. George is standing in line, his eyes glassy, gripping his empty plate. Pru turns to say something to him, then just... collapses into herself. Sean comes up next to them and grabs George's plate, filling it with food for him and guiding them to the table. Andrea follows, lost.

"How much longer until the bus leaves?" George asks as he sits down. "I think I need to go back and lie down."

Around us, the last scraps of normal burn out fast. Reality crashes back over us.

Harder. Heavier.

Unavoidable.

***

We're finishing the last zip lines when a scream rips through the air, raw and terrified.

We all freeze. My body locks up against my will, and I'm rooted to my spot. All I can smell is sweat, all I can hear are the insects around us, and I can't fucking move.

"No." George's whole body starts to quake. Sean grabs him before he can collapse.

Claire digs her nails into Riley's arm hard enough to make Riley wince.

Andrea and Pru are already across the other platform from where the sound came. It has to be one of them.

I finally snap out of it and force my body to move. The others follow quickly behind me.

We shove past people, clambering back down the tree, slipping and stumbling, and sprinting to the other side.

Andrea is standing there, white as a sheet. Pru is kneeling beside a woman writhing on the ground, clutching her calf.

"What the fuck happened?" I gasp as we skid to a stop.

"There was a spider." Andrea's voice shakes. Her eyes are locked on the woman, huge with shock.

Two guides push past us, taking over. Pru staggers back toward our group, breathing hard.

She turns on me, and I see it: the fire, the fury — the need to hurt someone.

"What about this, Lex?" she hisses. "Another accident? Or another attack?"

Her words hit hard like a punch to the gut.

I bite my tongue before I say something I'll regret. Then I turn and head for the bus before anyone sees me break.

***

Our group is dead silent on the way back to the ship.

What is there to say?

Riley sits next to me, her hair hanging in her face, but I can still see the tears tracking down her cheeks. George leans against the window, looking half-dead, as if he closes his eyes long enough, maybe none of this will be real. Claire is trying to comfort Pru, but all I can feel are her eyes glaring daggers at my head. Andrea and Sean hold hands quietly.

Hannah's death has shattered us.

And sitting here now, staring at the wreckage, I don't know how we're supposed to crawl out of it. I need to figure this out before whatever's left of us tears itself apart.

Riley rests her head on my shoulder, and I deflate.

We get back to the port, and Pru shoves people aside to rush off the bus and get back on the ship. Claire calls after her, trying to catch up. The rest of us walk slowly, feeling the dread of having to get back on the boat.

We make it through the checkpoint without a problem and start heading for the stairwell. There are too many people crammed together, and I can see George about to have an anxiety attack.

"Why don't we cut across the deck?" Andrea suggests quietly, seeing it too.

We slip onto the main deck and are about to cut across when my eyes snag on a commotion near another stairwell.

The medical team is dragging a teen from behind a door, bracing his neck and strapping him to a backboard.

He's not moving, and he is blue.

No. This cannot be happening again.

I slow, the world tilting. People are crowding the area, holding their breath.

And then — across the deck — my eyes meet his.

James.

He freezes as he sees me, and fear flickers across his face.

Fucking coward.

I hurl my bag at Riley and sprint.

Riley shouts. Andrea grabs for me, but misses.

It's too late.

I slam into James, driving him into the deck in a tackle.

This time, I'm not letting anyone get away.

Chapter Sixteen

"You fucking bastard!" I scream as my fist slams into James' face.

I straddle him, swinging wild, messy punches until my knuckles ache and his face blurs into something unrecognizable through my tears.

He fights back, but I don't feel it. My pulse pounds in my ears, drowning out the yelling and shouting around us.

It's like time has slowed down. I can't stop myself. I can see each hit land and recoil for another, even as the blood starts to pour from James' nose.

"Lexi! Fucking Christ, stop it!" James shouts, trying to fend me off.

I swing harder.

The stench of chlorine and salt fills my nose. Someone grabs my arm; I rip free. A woman tries to shove me off; I don't budge.

This is for Hannah. This is for everyone who won't make it home.

I've been patient long enough. No one else is doing anything.

Sean yanks me backward, his arms locking around my waist. I thrash against him, still clawing for James as Riley and Andrea rush to drag him up.

Sean is pushed off of me, and I can feel a hand grab my hair, another my arm, and cold metal bites into my wrists.

Handcuffs.

The music cuts out because of the commotion.

Noise floods back in, all of my senses finally catching up.

A rising tide of panic is crashing over me.

Everything blurs as I am dragged away.

***

For over an hour, I've been sitting in a metal chair in the brig, staring at the cell doors.

I could have killed him. I would have killed him if Sean hadn't stopped me.

Oh my God.

I feel the bile rise in my throat and have to choke it down.

"Lexi."

It's Theodore. His keys rattle as he unlocks the heavy door.

"Come on," he says as he opens the cell and leads me to a room. He doesn't look me in the eye as he keeps his distance.

I rub my wrists where the cuffs bit into them and sit in the chair offered to me. On the other side of the table, there's a man I don't know. I can tell he's tall and muscular. There's a coffee stain on the front of his shirt. His arms are crossed as he watches me sit down.

Theodore barely looks at me as he closes the door behind him and leaves, making me even more uneasy.

"Care to explain what happened earlier?" the man in the cof-fee-stained shirt says, gruffly, and his eye contact makes me want to shrink back.

I shrug. "Not really."

He sighs and steeples his hands, slow and deliberate. "We could keep you down here until we dock in New Orleans, if that's what you want."

I bark out a sharp, humorless laugh. "Of course. Jail the girl trying to stop a murderer. That makes sense."

His expression doesn't change. Not even a twitch.

"My friend is dead," I say, my voice low and shaking. "I think James did it. And no one's doing a goddamn thing."

He flips open a thin folder; Hannah's name is printed in neat, black letters.

"Hannah Maxwell," he says flatly. "Preliminary investigation shows that her death was a suicide."

The words land like a hammer to the chest.

No fucking way.

"You're full of shit," I snarl.

He closes the folder and fixes me with a dead-eyed glare. "We're trained to handle these things. Let us."

"Are you though?" I prod. "Because it looks like to me that you aren't trained to deal with anything. How many bodies have to pile up before you give a flying fuck?"

His eyes turn to stone as he stares at me, and his jaw clenches.

I hold his gaze in defiance.

Someone is killing people off, and no one will listen to me.

***

James refuses to press charges, and I am released late that afternoon with a warning that if security has to deal with me again, I'll be in the brig until the end of the cruise.

The sun is still shining, starkly contrasting with the dark and dimly lit cell I have been in. The light makes everything feel wrong, like nothing has happened, like things aren't completely falling apart everywhere I turn.

My hand throbs. Medical personnel shoved a cold pack at me, told me nothing was broken after they X-rayed my hand, and sent me on my way like I was some drunk asshole who got into a bar fight.

I wander back to our cabin, mindlessly passing people left and right.

It's dinner time, and I fully expect everyone to be eating after having not eaten much the past couple of days.

I enter the room and am swept up in a tight hug.

Riley.

They're all here, waiting for me.

"You guys didn't have to wait for me." I clear my throat. "I didn't think they were going to let me go."

"What the fuck, dude?" Pru snarls.

And that does it.

"Goddammit, Pru," I shout. "Can you fucking try to see this from where I'm standing for once?"

"Lexi—" George tries to cut in.

"No," Pru barks, "because I'm not a fucking psychopath!"

The room freezes.

The fire in my veins is reignited.

I walk up to her and look her in the eye. "You know as well as I do that Hannah wouldn't kill herself," I say dangerously under my breath.

George slams his fist into the wall, a loud boom in the room's tension. "Now you *all* sound crazy!" He screams. "Why can't you just leave it be?"

He storms out of the room and slams the door behind him.

None of us moves.

"I agree with Lex," Riley finally breaks the silence. "Hannah wouldn't do that."

"Can you not see what's happening here? They're picking us off—one by one. Making us tear each other apart so we don't notice who's next," I say, low and determined.

"Lexi," Andrea approaches me and touches my shoulders. "What do you want us to do?"

Sean and Claire nod behind her in agreement, but I see Pru shake her head, disgust on her face.

At least this is a start.

CHAPTER SEVENTEEN

Everyone's staring at me, waiting for an answer.

Pru's arms are locked across her chest, her whole body rigid with skepticism. She doesn't want to be here. She doesn't want to believe me.

"Why don't we go talk to Keith and Theodore?" I blurt out. My voice comes out too loud, too desperate. "Sit them down. Make them listen."

"Listen to *what*?" Pru snaps. "Lex, you don't have any proof."

I suck in a breath, a scream clawing its way up my throat that I have to choke down. "Pru, how could you even *think* Hannah would do this? There were no signs."

She throws her arms out, wild and angry. "This isn't some goddamn movie, Lexi! This is *real life*!"

Before I can tear into her, Andrea wedges herself between us, hands up. "Everyone *breathe*," she says sharply.

"There's gotta be surveillance footage," Riley cuts in. "We can ask them to pull it."

Claire nods, albeit hesitantly. "Yeah. That's smart."

Sean, sitting hollow-eyed, drags a hand through his hair. "I don't know, guys. George wouldn't want this."

"George doesn't know what the fuck he wants right now," I snap, and Sean flinches like I hit him.

Pru rounds on me, raw and furious. "Oh, and you do?"

Claire grabs Pru's hand, squeezing. "Babe. Stop. Either help us, or don't, but stop tearing Lexi apart."

Pru yanks her hand away with a sharp breath. "I need some air."

Claire lets her go, but her voice is firm. "Fine. But not alone. On the balcony. Now."

The door clicks shut behind Pru. The silence after is suffocating.

"George is alone," Sean whispers, voice breaking. "I should check on him."

Andrea's already moving. "I'm coming with you," she says. No argument.

"Check in every ten minutes," Riley says, sharp and steady. They both nod before slipping out.

The door closes again, leaving just the three of us. Riley, Claire, and I are all staring at each other.

Claire rubs her hands down her thighs, restless. "How the hell do we even find Keith and Theodore?"

"Guest services?" Riley offers, voice tight.

Claire doesn't answer right away. She's staring out at Pru, who's pacing the balcony.

"I'll stay here," Claire says finally. "See if I can calm her down." She lets out a rough sigh. "I've never seen her like this. She's... she's just so angry."

She isn't the only one.

I can feel the anger simmering in my veins.

I want answers. I want to know what the fuck is happening on this boat.

Riley stands up and offers her hand. I take it and lace our fingers together, my grip tight.

"Ten minutes and we'll message you an update. Don't leave this room." I speak.

Hopefully, Claire can keep Pru from completely breaking.

***

We tear through the halls toward guest services, earning strange looks along the way from the other passengers.

I'm sure we look like hell. My clothes are still rumpled from the holding cell, and Riley's covered in dirt and sweat from zip-lining, but I don't give a single fuck.

We reach guest services, and Linda is at the counter.

Of course, she looks like she'd rather be anywhere but here.

Her mouth tightens the second she sees us.

"If you cause a scene again, I *will* call security," she warns, voice already weary.

Riley flashes her a sweet, fake-ass smile. "Actually, that's exactly what we want."

Linda blinks dumbly, thrown off. "What for?"

I slam my palms down on the counter, hard enough to make her jump. "None of your fucking business," I snarl. "Either you help us, or I swear to God, lady, I will make you wish you had."

Her eyes dart to Riley, maybe hoping for a buffer, but Riley shrugs.

"Get security," Riley says pleasantly. "We'll wait."

Linda scrambles for the phone.

Good. For once, someone else can be afraid.

Moments later, a bald, overweight security officer approaches us, glaring.

I frown and sigh. "Of course. The one time we need Keith or Theodore," I mumble to Riley. "Good evening, sir." I grimace at him.

He grunts and motions for us to follow—no cuffs yet, so that's a good sign. We exchange a glance and obey, fast enough to keep the peace, but slow enough to show we're not scared.

Not anymore.

***

Riley and I find Keith and Theodore, but they seem less than pleased that we are again in their interrogation room. They sit down, arms crossed, expressions hard as stone.

"Let me get this straight," Keith begins. "You thought it would be a good idea to harass poor Linda, *again*, I might add, after the shitshow you got yourself involved in today?"

"How's the hand, Rocky?" Theodore deadpans.

I flex my fingers without thinking. The pain, pushed aside for hours, throbs back to life. I smirk anyway. "Still better than James' face."

Keith leans forward, cutting through the banter. "Why are you here, Alexandria?"

Riley shifts in her chair, but her voice is steady. "Murder."

I bark a harsh, humorless laugh — it bursts out before I can stop it. "What my very subtle girlfriend here means," I say, "is that we want to see the surveillance footage. From every death on this ship." I grab her hand in solidarity.

The room goes still.

Keith and Theodore look at each other for the first time since we sat down. And that, that tiny flicker of hesitation, tells me everything.

There's something they're not saying.

"We can't release that to you," Keith says, "but know that we have gone over every inch of it, and we haven't found anything out of the ordinary."

"So it's ordinary for this many people to die on a cruise? They should put that in their brochures." I sneer.

"You'd better watch yourself," Theodore says, his eyes flashing momentarily.

I raise a brow, unafraid. "You're right, I'd better watch myself or I'll end up fucking dead like the other, how many people are there now? And what about the missing couple?"

I stand up and slap my hands on the desk. "Why won't you admit that something is happening and we need to watch our backs?"

Riley's eyes are as wide as saucers as she tries to grab my arm. I wrench it away and point my finger in the men's faces. "Or maybe that's exactly what you want—for us to 'trust' you so you can pull the rug out from under us."

Theodore stands up and grabs my wrist.

Harsh. Bruising.

"Listen here," he hisses through clenched teeth. "I know that your friend is dead, but that doesn't give you an excuse to act like a fucking child."

"Theodore. Sit your ass back down," Keith roars, shaking the walls, as I yank my arm back at the same time Theodore shoves, making me stumble.

I crash into Riley, her arms locking around me before I hit the floor.

"I knew you were playing too calm," I bare my teeth at the younger officer.

I see it now, his cracks.

"Lexi, please stop," Riley whispers in my ear.

I can't.

People are dead.

Hannah is dead.

I won't fucking stop until I burn this shit to the ground.

***

The door slams shut behind us, the glass rattling in its frame.

Riley snags my arm. I tear free without thinking.

"Did you see that shit?" I snarl, rounding on her. "They're not here to help us at all."

I catch a security officer coming down the hall and slow clap at him. "Great fucking job. A-plus work you guys are doing." Venom drips from every word.

Riley smacks my hands down and pushes me to keep walking.

"What the fuck is wrong with you?" she hisses, looking behind her at the officer, as she shoves me down the hall. "Lexi, *breathe.*"

I whirl on her so fast she stumbles back.

"I can't fucking breathe!" I yell, the sound ricocheting down the corridor. "Everything is falling apart, and you want me to *breathe*?"

Riley recoils, and the look on her face makes me freeze.

Wide eyes stare at me, her mouth hanging open.

I stagger back like I've been punched in the stomach.

"I'm sorry," I rasp. "Fuck. I'm sorry."

I move closer, hands half-raised in surrender.

She takes a step back.

"Are you..." I swallow hard. "Are you afraid of me?"

Riley shakes her head too fast, too hard. "No. Of course not. But Lexi..." She lets out a shaky breath. "I've never seen you like this."

Before I can respond, our phones both go off.

"Fuck, we didn't message them." I groan and check our group message.

Where the hell are you guys? - Claire

We're in George's room. - Andrea

No, Lexi and Riley. They've been gone for 45 minutes. - Pru

Riley's already firing off a reply. I can't even move.

We're fine. We're on our way back. - Riley

Riley slips her phone into her pocket and looks at me with an unreadable expression I have never seen before. "We need to go." Her voice is flat, defeated.

I nod, numb. "Okay."

My rage deflates as I follow Riley, who is tense and has her head held high.

I know that posture.

She's protecting herself.

From me.

CHAPTER EIGHTEEN

Riley and I trek back to our cabin in suffocating silence. She's one step ahead of me, keeping me at a distance.

Not that I can blame her.

My mind whirls with everything that happened as I watch her rigid posture and hands balled into fists.

I've never felt so far away from her. And it's all my fault.

We make it to the room, and she shoves the keycard in the door and flings it open. She doesn't wait for me to follow her before the door starts to close, and I rush inside before it slams in my face.

We barely make it inside before we're bombarded with questions.

"What happened?" Andrea demands, eyes wide and frantic.

Claire barrels toward us, hope lighting up her face. "Did they get anything? Tell me they got something."

Pru's jaw is clenched tight. "Please, God, tell me they didn't just blow you off."

Their questions hit me like shots in the heart.

I can't breathe.

Riley answers before I can even open my mouth. "Nothing," she says, her voice razor-sharp. "They gave us nothing but a slap on the wrist like we were two fucking toddlers."

Without another word, she storms through the cabin and yanks open the balcony door so hard it bangs against the wall. The doorframe rattles when she slams it shut behind her.

I jolt at the violence of the sound.

Andrea whirls to me, wide-eyed. "What the fuck happened?"

My eyes fill with frustrated tears. "Can you guys... can you just give us a few minutes?"

Dejected, the group leaves the room, talking amongst themselves. Andrea pauses in the doorway and gives me one last look before she nods.

I take a deep breath and steel myself before opening the balcony door and standing in the doorway.

Riley is standing at the railing, her jaw set and eyes ablaze. She turns to me and stalks toward me like a panther does its prey.

"Do not *ever* do that again, do you hear me?" She hisses through clenched teeth. My eyes widen as she gets closer to me, her chest heaving. "Do not ever take your anger out on me again."

I nod, my body trembling.

Then she grabs my hair, yanking me into a rough kiss.

It's bruising, and it's exactly what I need.

I slam her against the balcony window, and she lets out a loud moan.

I fumble the door open and push her backward into the room, not breaking the kiss as I follow.

My shirt is gone before I can register it, and Riley rips hers off too, tossing it across the room. Her bra follows, furiously, and then she shoves me backward onto the bed.

I land hard, the mattress bouncing under me.

She strips her shorts and underwear off in one frantic motion, kicking them away without care.

And then she's on me, straddling my lap, naked, her knees digging into the bed on either side of my hips.

"Please." She begs against my lips. "Please, Lex."

She rolls her hips, attempting to find friction, her eyes wild as she breaks the kiss and looks at me.

I can feel her trembling.

I reach down and feel her wetness, making us both gasp. I enter her with two fingers and start a brutal pace.

Head thrown back, she gasps, exposing the line of her throat.

I nip and suck and bite as I move my fingers inside of her.

Warm. Wet.

Tight.

She sobs, arching into me, riding my fingers. I feel her clench around me, already close.

I slow my thrusts, twisting my fingers, and she moans, low and broken.

"I love you," I whisper against her throat.

That's all it takes.

She shatters in my arms, crying out as she comes hard around my fingers.

Her body crumples against me. Trembling and wrecked.

I slip my hand free and hold her as she sobs against my chest, all the fight and fury drained out of her.

"I'm so sorry," I murmur into her hair, kissing her forehead, closed eyelids, and lips. "I'm so, so sorry."

I can feel her heart pounding against my chest as she clings to me.

My heartbeat matches hers, beat for beat.

***

We lay there for a while, the silence less suffocating than earlier, as Riley holds onto me like she's afraid to let go.

I rub slow, shaky circles along her bare arm, grounding both of us.

"We need to get up and talk to everyone," I finally murmur, my throat raw.

"Can we just stay here the rest of the trip?" she whispers. "Can we pretend this has all been a bad dream?"

Her fingers tighten against my ribs.

I close my eyes, wishing I could give her that. Wishing we could hide here, in the ruins of everything.

But we can't.

"We have to stop this," I whisper back. "Before it happens to someone else."

Riley lets out a long, broken sigh and sits up.

The sheets fall away from her body, and for a second, I just drink her in — alive, breathing, here.

"I'll message the others," she says, glancing at the clock. "We all need to eat something. We can regroup over dinner."

I nod, even though every part of me wants to pull her back into bed and pretend nothing exists beyond these walls.

***

We make our way through the ship's halls, walking side by side, the familiar buzz of anxiety rising in my chest.

I scan the passing crew members as they rush around, my heart pounding.

"What's going on?" I mutter, half-dreading the answer.

Please, God, not another death.

Riley stops a passing crew member.

"Big storm coming," they explain quickly. "Tomorrow's party got moved up to tonight."

Then they hurry off, leaving us standing there.

Riley exhales slowly. "Just a storm."

"Yeah," I mutter. "'Cause that's what we need right now."

We keep moving and finally make it to the dining room, where everyone but George is already gathered around a long table.

Sean has a panicked look on his face, tearing his beverage napkin to shreds. Surprisingly, it's Pru talking him down.

"There's a storm coming," he squeaks when he sees us.

"We heard." I nod and look around, putting on a strong front in front of my friends.

Andrea is staring off into space, and I sit down across from her, waving my hand in front of her. "Earth to Dre."

Her eyes snap into focus, and she glances at me before breaking eye contact. The cracks are getting deeper, and her face is drawn in worry. "Sorry. What's up?" Her eyes are glassy, and she looks like she hasn't slept in days.

I smile at her sympathetically. "Nothing, just checking on you."

George pops up behind us and sits down. "There's a party tonight." He takes a deep breath. "I think we should go."

"George-" Claire starts, but he holds up his hand.

"All I want right now is to get fucked up," he says, voice cracking, "and pretend my girlfriend and unborn child aren't dead."

The dining room buzzes with noise, oblivious. At our table, only the echo of George's voice lingers.

"Whatever you want, George," I place a hand on his arm, helpless to do anything else.

CHAPTER NINETEEN

The deck's music was so loud that people had to yell to be heard over it, and it rattled the bones in her body.

The night's party was in full swing, and the drinks had been flowing for hours. People were dancing, laughing, and having a good time, but she needed to escape.

She needed a moment to herself.

She stumbled up the stairs, swiping at her cheeks with the heel of her hand, hating that she was crying again.

A broken gasp passed her lips as she made her way to a dark corner, needing the reprieve from the noise and people.

The noise dulled to a heavy thud in the shadows near the railing. She braced herself on the cool metal, chest heaving, staring at the endless black water.

"Don't feel like partying?" A voice asked from behind her.

She spun, a hand to her chest. She could make out the outline of a person, half in the shadows, the dark hiding most of their body.

"No." She scowled, her heart pounding in her chest. "I'm trying to get some quiet for a moment, if you don't mind."

They shrugged. "I can be quiet."

She looked at them, really looked at them, and a shiver ran through her.

"No, thank you. I'll be back down in a few minutes," she said firmly.

The person smiled slowly, almost lazily. "Fair enough." They walked away, humming under their breath.

She waited until they disappeared around the corner before exhaling.

Her hands were shaking.

She felt the chill in the air and hugged herself, glancing over her shoulder to make sure they had walked away.

With one last sigh, she pushed off the railing and headed to the staircase to return to the party.

A footstep behind her.

And another.

The squeak of a shoe gave the person away.

Whirling around, she came face to face with them.

"You know," they said, voice low and almost thoughtful, "it's rude to tell someone to fuck off like that."

The pain hit like a lightning strike. She gasped, hands trembling, vision tunneling in. She looked down. The knife, Jesus, the knife, was buried deep in her ribs, handle already slick with her blood.

"Wha-"

"Shhh." They put a finger to her lips.

She reacted without thinking; the only thing on her mind was getting away.

She forced herself down the stairs behind her. Bloodied handprints were left behind on the shining metal. The spatter on the deck was like gunshots in the air.

The blade ground against her ribs with every breath, fire racing up her spine.

The last few steps disappeared under her feet as her hands slipped in the slick blood left behind. She crashed hard onto the lower deck, landing in a twisted heap.

For a second, she heard nothing—only the roar of her own heartbeat.

Then screams.

Someone is shouting for help.

Hands on her shoulders, voices rising in panic.

She tried to lift her head. She opened her mouth to scream.

Blood bubbled up her throat, drowning the sound.

The world spun once, violently, and everything went black.

CHAPTER TWENTY

The moment we step onto the deck, the noise slams into us. The DJ is blasting a Top 100 hit, people are laughing and dancing, and drinks are flowing like nothing in the world could ever go wrong.

And for them, it hasn't. They don't realize there are ghosts among us.

Lines at the bars stretch five deep, bartenders scrambling to keep up. We weave through the crush of bodies, each grabbing two drinks to avoid the lines again, and somehow George scores an open table near the DJ booth.

The crowd is packed in tight, the air heavy with heat and the storm rolling in. Every breath feels like a fight.

George bobs his head to the beat, smiling, laughing, but it's an act. I can see it in how his eyes stay flat and he finishes his first drink in two desperate gulps before tearing into the second.

I sip mine slowly, my nerves fraying with every second.

A hand slips into mine, steady and familiar.

Riley watches George with a quiet sadness before turning to me, offering a small, broken smile. "Let's just pretend," she says. "For at least the next hour. Let's pretend we're normal people, partying on a cruise."

Her fingers tighten around mine, and I let myself believe her for a moment.

Just for a moment.

I tip my drink back, finishing it, and let her drag me into the mass of bodies. The lights strobe over the dance floor, flashing over the rest of the group as they join us.

Out of the corner of my eye, I catch George laughing, a little too loudly, as Sean struggles to keep hold of his drinks, his face a miserable shade of green.

And for the first time in what feels like forever, a real laugh bubbles up inside me.

I grab Riley around the waist and bring her closer to me, planting a quick kiss on her lips, as we move to the song's rhythm.

I feel a tap on my shoulder and turn my head to find Pru behind me. "Can we talk?" Her shoulders hunch.

I nod, brush a kiss against Riley's temple, and let Claire slide into my place without missing a beat. Pru and I drift to the outer edge of the party, where the music is a little less deafening.

I cross my arms and wait.

She shifts from one foot to the other. "Lex, I'm sorry. I haven't been fair to you. Claire's been riding my ass all day," she mutters, looking out over the dark water. "Telling me you're right. Telling me Hannah would never... that she wouldn't..." She sucks in a breath. "I didn't want to believe it. Because if you're right, then someone is killing people off. And we're trapped out here, with nowhere to run."

Her voice breaks on the last words.

I lay a hand on her arm, a gentle squeeze, because what the hell else is there to say?

"I know," I whisper. "I know."

She drags her eyes back to me, and there's steel in them now. "Whatever you need," she says. "I'm with you. I'm sorry it took me this long."

I nod and pull her into a hug. She nearly crushes me.

"Right now, we pretend," I murmur. "For George. For Riley. For Claire. But later..." I pull back, eyes steady. "Later, I'm going to need you."

Pru nods, fierce and confident, and we return to the group.

When we reach them, Riley pulls her into a hug, laughing into her ear. I can't hear the words, but Pru laughs too. Smiles like she's trying to believe it.

George is holding two fresh drinks.

I sigh.

***

I promised Riley an hour, and that's what I gave her. One hour to act like our entire lives weren't breaking apart at the seams. When the hour ends, I slip away, mumbling about needing the bathroom.

No one questions it.

I don't head for the bathroom. I don't even know where I'm going.

There are still a fair number of people inside who don't want to join the party on the deck, and I can't blame them. I can still hear the music even in the halls.

"Lexi," a voice calls out from behind me.

It's Theodore, and my heart begins to race. The bruises on my arm from earlier throb at the sight of him.

"Theodore." I greet the man, bracing myself.

"Don't feel like partying?" he asks, and I shake my head. He sighs and looks around him. "I want to apologize for earlier. I lost my cool, and that was... unprofessional."

I raise a brow. "There's a lot of that going around tonight." I look around him. "Where's your partner?"

Theodore shrugs. "We split up because of the party." He stands there casually, but I can see the tension in his shoulders.

"Uh huh." I nod, not letting my eyes leave him.

He finally relaxes. "Anyway, I saw you and wanted to come say that." He nods his head and turns away from me.

I should let him walk away.

"I'm not wrong," I say, my voice cutting through the hall.

He stops and slowly turns back.

"Someone's killing people," I continue, "and it's not over."

"I hope for all of our sakes that you're wrong." He says and turns, walking off without looking back

I watch him retreat, something nagging in my mind, but I can't pinpoint it. Before I can analyze the thought further, my phone buzzes in my pocket.

Did you fall in? Do you need a hand? ;) - Riley

I didn't expect to be missed so quickly, and I sigh with resignation as I head back onto the deck.

***

I bump into Andrea before I see anyone else. She staggers, catching herself on my shoulder, her eyes glassy and unfocused.

"Lexi!" She burps, and the smell of tequila attacks me. "Where did you go? We're doing limbo."

My eyes widen in horror. "How much have you had to drink?"

"Enough to try to forget about this fucking vacation." She slurs and lifts her chin defiantly. "Everything has gone to such shit."

She almost falls over, and I slide my arm around her to catch her. Her eyes fill with tears, and I take a deep breath. "Where's Sean?"

"He's dancing with George," she hiccups. "Oh, George."

I drag Dre with me as I search for the rest of our friends. Sure enough, a limbo bar is set up, and Claire is trying to get under it without touching it. She falls on her ass with a loud laugh, standing up and throwing herself at Pru.

"Rye," I shout over the music, and her head snaps up.

"Hi, babe!" She waves at me.

I was gone for twenty minutes. Twenty minutes, and everyone is unraveling.

"Lex, guess what?" Pru grins lazily at me. "Claire and I are getting married."

Andrea gasps dramatically and tackles both in a hug, making them a mess of arms and giving them sloppy kisses on the cheeks.

I'm rooted to my spot. Stunned.

"I thought—" I start, turning to Claire, but she's already shaking her head, wide-eyed and desperate.

Pru catches it, of course. "What?" she demands, frowning.

"Nothing, baby," Claire says quickly, kissing Pru's cheek. "Come on, let's find the boys."

She tries to herd her away, but it's too late. The moment's cracked open.

We round the corner just in time to see Sean hunched over a trash can, throwing up, while   George dances drunken circles around him, his smile wide and manic and his eyes hollow.

"Oh, baby," Andrea cries, falling to her knees beside Sean and rubbing his back.

Pru glances back at me, suspicion sharpening her drunken haze. "What were you going to say, Lexi?"

Shit.

Riley cuts in, her voice too loud and too bright. "What my lovely girlfriend meant to say is congratulations!"

Everything stops.

George freezes mid-step. It's like his body stops in its tracks against his will.

"Congratulations on what?" he slurs, blinking at us.

The boat rocks under his feet, or maybe that's just him swaying from the alcohol.

No one answers.

"Guys," George says, voice cracking. "Tell me."

With Pru staring expectantly at her, Claire's mouth works silently before she whispers, "We're getting married."

It feels like a bomb.

George reels back like she slapped him. "What?"

"Claire and I are getting married," Pru repeats.

George's face crumples, grief and rage colliding all at once.

"Are you fucking kidding me?" he spits, stumbling forward. His face is red and blotchy. "Hannah's not even cold, and you're out here celebrating?"

Claire shrinks back, tears flooding her eyes. "We were going to wait," she chokes out. "I didn't want—"

"Wait for what?" George roars. "For us to bury her? For me to just get over the fact that my pregnant girlfriend is dead?"

"You didn't want what?" Pru scoffs at Claire.

The music continues to thump. Around us, people are still oblivious.

In our little circle, everything is collapsing.

"Fuck you," spittle flies from George's mouth. "Hannah would still be here if it weren't for you all."

George storms off, and Andrea is the one to follow him, calling after him.

Sean stands from his crouched position and wipes his mouth. "Congratulations," he says, his throat raw, before he follows George and Andrea.

Again, we're divided.

Again, we're angry at each other.

Pru and Claire separate and stand apart, heads both down.

"I'll be back." Claire wipes a tear. "I have to go to the restroom."

"I'll come with you," Riley offers.

"No, I'm fine." Claire puts a hand up. "Just give me a minute."

I'm the only one who notices that she walks off opposite the bathroom, and I have half a mind to follow her.

Pru looks between us, and she walks off as well.

***

Riley and I find a chair and squeeze into it. The party continues around us, and the atmosphere feels wrong for what transpired between us.

Riley opens her mouth to say something, but then screams tear through the air.

I'm on my feet instantly and running toward the sound, Riley at my side.

We shove through the crowd, sprinting toward the staircase where people are backing away, faces reflecting horror.

I see George. His eyes are filled with tears.

And then I realize...

He's standing with a knife, droplets of blood dripping onto the deck.

Pru is crumpled on the ground, a dark pool growing around her.

Her chest is spattered red.

The wet, awful sound of breath struggling through blood.

Pru's eyes meet mine.

My heart feels like it's stopped. She's going to die right in front of us, and there's nothing I can do.

My legs move before my brain can process, and I'm on the floor, pressing down on the stab wound in Pru's chest.

"Goddammit, Pru," I sob. "Stay with me."

Chaos explodes around us.

Riley is screaming at George, who drops the knife and backs away, hands held up in the air.

"You fucking bastard!" she shouts, charging him and punching him in the face, dropping him to the deck.

"Lex—" Pru gurgles, blood pooling in her throat, her eyes locked on mine in terror.

"Shh." I gasp. "Don't try to talk. I've got you."

My head whips up to the crowd around us. "Don't just stand there! Do something!"

Keith rushes around the corner and drops to his knees beside me. His hands cover mine, smearing blood everywhere.

"I've got her." He pants. "Lexi, I've got her."

I nod and fall back, putting Pru's head in my lap. Her arm lifts, weakly, and I grip her hand tight.

Two other officers have George on the ground, arms wrenched behind his back as he yells and thrashes. Andrea, Sean, and Claire rush up behind me.

Claire's scream is inhuman, ripping across the deck. She drops beside us, her hand trembling as it finds Pru's hair. "Baby, look at me." She's shaking violently. "*Look at me!*"

Pru turns to look at her and coughs up more blood. It trickles thickly down the side of her mouth.

"Claire." Pru chokes, tears spilling down her face. "I love you."

"You can't leave me!" Claire howls. "We're getting married. We're supposed to grow old together."

Medical staff rush to us, trying to push us out of the way. Claire refuses to move.

Pru's eyes start to close, and Claire cradles her cheek. "Pru, don't close your eyes. Don't you *dare* close your eyes."

Keith staggers to his feet, hands covered in blood, as he stares at us in shock.

Pru's eyes stay on Claire as her body begins to shake. "Claire," she sobs, a last breath catching. Her body goes limp in my hands, her grip on my hand slackening.

I shake as I hold her. My breath comes in broken gasps.

No. Claire is wailing, raw and devastated. Riley pulls her back, giving the medics room, but it's too late.

Pru is dead.

Claire collapses into Riley. Andrea doubles over, a guttural cry tearing from her. Sean clutches his chest like he's been stabbed, too.

And George.

He's still thrashing, trying to fight the officers pinning him down.

I gently lay Pru's head down. My fingers tremble. Blood streaks my palms.

I rise and begin to walk.

"Lexi, get back!" Keith yells, now helping to hold George down.

Dropping down, I meet George's eye.

"I will make you pay, you fucking son of a bitch."

Chapter Twenty-One

In the aftermath, the party has officially been disbanded. George has been hauled away, screaming the whole time that he didn't do anything. Keith watches us closely, asking basic questions to which there's no good answer.

Pru's body is on the deck, covered by a sheet, the bloodstain from her chest soaking through the white. It's a ghastly reminder of her horrific death.

"Lexi, Riley," Keith's voice cuts through the fog in my mind. "You two said you were here before anyone else. What did you see?"

Riley swallows hard. "George was standing over her with a knife," she whispers.

Looking at my hands, they're still stained with blood. My heart pounds. "How could he?" I look up at Keith, lost. "How the fuck could he do this?"

I feel the bile rising in my throat, and I'm helpless to stop it as I run to a trash can and empty my stomach.

The deck is crawling with security, questioning the people who were near the staircase when Pru died. I can hear snippets of what others are saying as I straighten and wipe my mouth with the back of my hand, not caring about the blood.

The deck spins sickly around me, the bile still sour on my tongue. My eyes trail over everyone as I try to focus on what's being said.

"He was standing over her and drove the knife in," one lady slurs.

A man, eyes skittish, says, "I only saw him standing over her with the knife."

"She fell down the stairs, and the knife was already there." I whip my head around, stunned. A woman is shaking and talking to one of the officers. "That man ran up, shouted, then pulled the knife out."

I bolt over to her and grab her arm. "What did you just say?" I ask, low and threatening.

She looks at me, wide-eyed. "What?"

The officer sighs. "Ma'am, I need you to step back. We're conducting an investigation."

"No fucking shit," I spit out and keep my eyes trained on her. "You said she was already stabbed?"

She looks around nervously. "Yes? I saw her fall from the stairs, and the knife was already there."

"Ma'am." The security guard waves Keith over. "I need you to back away."

Keith approaches and places a gentle hand on my shoulder. "Lexi, let them do their jobs."

I shrug Keith off and put my hands up in surrender, tearing my eyes away from her and stalking back to the group. Andrea and Sean are pale, their eyes glazed over. Riley is holding   Claire, who looks catatonic. Riley and I make eye contact, and she slightly shakes her head, giving Claire what's meant to be a comforting squeeze. Claire is still unmoving.

"Let's get you out of here," Keith says quietly. "You don't need to see any more of this. We'll have to talk to each of you downstairs, but we can get you somewhere more comfortable for now."

He guides us into the ship and down to the blocked library area. Not one word has been spoken between us as we process what happened.

***

Once again, I find myself in the brig. Instead of the small interrogation room, I am in a bigger room so more officers can fit. There are four of them: two supervisors and two officers who were on the upper deck. Keith is one of them. I don't know the others.

"Can you tell us what happened tonight?" Another muscular man, hair in a crew cut with sharp features, stares hard at me.

His nameplate fittingly reads *Briggs,* and he's the Chief of Security.

I tip my head back, and my focus is drawn to a stain on the ceiling. The stain is dark and shaped like Snoopy. It's ridiculous, a stupid thing to fixate on, but I can't stop staring at it.

I let the events of the night wash over me. I involuntarily shiver, remembering Pru's panicked look before the light in them went out. My eyes fill with tears, and I choke back a sob.

"Lexi," Keith prods.

I take a deep breath and gaze at the men before me. They all look expectant, which angers m ven more.

Pru is dead. Hannah is dead. And they want to ask what happened?

"You tell me," I say.

One of the officers raises an eyebrow. "You were there. We need witness statements."

"My friend just died in my arms," I snarl. "After one of my other friends allegedly killed herself. I think you should be asking bigger questions."

"And what should we be asking?" Briggs asks, raising a hand to silence the officer beside him.

I lean forward and lock eyes with each of them, my fists balling tight.

A beat passes. No one speaks. "I think you should be asking why so many people keep dying under your watch."

"Ma'am-"

"Do *not* patronize me," I warn the officer and shoot out of my seat. "I've seen it, right in front of my fucking eyes. People are dying left and right, and you can't tell me they were all accidents."

Keith stands and walks over to me, and I shrug off his hand, which he tries to put on my shoulder.

"Keith, seriously. You've been there for almost all of them," I stop as a horrifying thought hits me. "Why are you always there?" I step back from the man, trying to create distance between us.

"Lexi, please sit down." One of the officers tries to gently tell me, but I can see no emotion in his eyes.

I don't sit, and I turn to walk towards the door. "Am I free to go?"

"You're not being detained, if that's what you're asking," Keith replies.

Theodore comes into the room, and I have to jump out of the way of the door opening. He walks straight to Briggs and leans down to whisper something in his ear.

Briggs stands up, and Theodore's eyes widen when he finally notices me, like he didn't realize I was in the room.

"Lexi, unless you have anything to add, you're free to go," Briggs announces, as if I didn't just witness the hurried exchange between them.

"What happened?" I ask.

Theodore sighs. "There's footage-"

"Theodore!" Briggs says firmly and shakes his head. He turns to me. "We will let you know our findings once the investigation is over."

"Surveillance footage?" I don't give up. "What about all of the other deaths? Did you find the footage for those, too?"

"Lexi, please." Keith sighs. "Let us do our job. I'll tell you what we find once the investigation is complete, even though it breaks policy."

My jaw clenches, and I know I won't get anywhere with these men. Not right now.

"Fine." I grit out and turn to the door again. I make it halfway before spinning back to face Briggs. "Why has the Coast Guard not been called in for this?"

Theodore rolls his eyes. "You watch too many movies, Lexi."

Keith shoots him a look that makes him deflate. "We've been in contact with them. They're aware of what's going on. Up until now, there's been no reason to believe that any of the deaths have been suspicious. We will inform them of this situation and let them decide how to handle it from here."

I nod. "Fine. But I'm telling you, those other deaths? They weren't accidents. They were murder."

CHAPTER TWENTY-TWO

I'm escorted back to the closed-off library where the rest of the group waits. The moment I see Riley, I walk straight to her and wrap her in a hug. My hand finds the back of her head as I hold her tight, clinging to the only comfort I have left. She sniffles against my ear, and it takes everything in me not to completely fall apart.

"Are you okay?" Riley whispers. I nod and pull back, brushing a tear from her cheek with my thumb.

"Claire Jennings?" An officer, Smith, calls out, and I cringe.

Claire is curled on the couch, flanked by Andrea and Sean. Her legs are tucked up to her chest, chin resting on her knees. Her eyes are so vacant, I swear the ship could sink and she wouldn't notice. The room is warm, but goosebumps line her bare arms.

"Can you please give her some time?" Andrea asks before anyone else can. "She just lost her girlfriend." She glances over at Claire. "I don't think she is in any place to be talking about anything."

"Fiancée," Riley corrects quietly. "She lost her fiancée."

The word hangs there, heavy.

No one speaks.

Sean and Andrea exchange a look. Then Sean stands. "Can you take me next?"

Smith grunts and jerks his head. "Let's go."

Sean follows him out without a glance back. I slide into his spot next to Claire.

She hasn't blinked since I walked in. Her eyes are wide and locked straight ahead, as if she's reliving over and over the moment her world changed forever.

I gently tuck a strand of hair behind her ear.

Nothing. No reaction.

I glance across her to Andrea, who shakes her head.

"She hasn't moved since she sat down. She hasn't said a single word," Andrea murmurs.

My eyes fill with tears, and I try to imagine the pain that Claire feels right now. I realize it's pointless, because I can't even begin to know what she is feeling. I put a hand over hers and squeeze, not expecting a response.

I don't get one.

We sit in silence as the officer continues to rotate through the room, taking statements individually. My mind won't stop running, replaying everything over and over again. I try to sit still to not disturb Claire, but my legs bounce in a nervous tic out of my control. Riley had stood up a while ago to browse the books, and after selecting one, she sat back down; it's been lying unopened on her lap for the past thirty minutes.

Andrea had been called after Sean, and he now paces through the small room, mumbling to himself and constantly running his hand through his hair.

Riley is called after Andrea, and I watch her go, my heart breaking even more at her downturned shoulders as she follows the officer.

I barely have any time to process what is happening when the next instant, she is hurling obscenities, and the officer grabs her around the waist to haul her back.

Andrea and I shoot to our feet and immediately see what set her off. George.

Another officer is escorting him to the library, and Riley is still attempting to reach him.

"You fucking prick!" she screams, clawing at the arms around her waist.

George's eyes are wide as saucers, and he ducks behind the officer beside him, just as Riley breaks free and lunges.

"Ma'am!" someone shouts as she's tackled and slammed to the floor.

"Hey!" Sean bellows, making a beeline for the officer pinning her down.

"We need some help up here!" One of the officers barks into his radio.

"Get the fuck off of her!" I yell, pushing forward as Sean and I both try to yank the officer off Riley.

The stomping of footsteps echoes in the hall before Keith and Theodore jump into the chaos.

"Higgens! Get off her!" Keith goes to the officer on Riley and pulls him up.

Riley springs to her feet, fire in her eyes, as she glares at Higgens. She brushes herself off before her eyes dart to George. She makes another move toward him, but Theodore stops her.

"Riley, stop for a moment," he commands.

Riley listens, but her fists are clenched at her side, and she vibrates with barely contained rage.

"What the fuck is going on?" I demand. "Why is he here?"

Keith turns to the officer with George and gives him a scathing look. "You couldn't bring him somewhere else? Are you kidding me?"

The officer has the decency to flush and avert his eyes.

"Guys, I can explain," George begs, holding his hands up with tears in his eyes.

"There will never be an explanation for what you did," Andrea says.

"Let him explain," a broken voice says from behind us, and we all turn to watch Claire. She has her arms wrapped around herself and is staring directly at George. "Let him explain how he took my entire life from me, " she rasps, her voice barely audible over her grief.

George's face crumples, but before he can speak, Keith answers.

"We watched the surveillance footage." He clears his throat. "Pru had already been stabbed when George reached her. He was trying to help her by pulling out the knife." He shakes his head. "Nothing anyone could have done would have made a difference. Her wound was too extensive."

"So who fucking stabbed her then?" Riley asks.

Keith shifts uncomfortably, and Theodore speaks up. "We don't know. There was no footage of where the incident occurred."

"No footage?" I scoff and look suspiciously at all the officers. "That's fucking convenient."

"It's not that there is no footage; it must have happened in a blind spot where the camera didn't pick anything up." Keith clarifies.

"How is that even possible?" Sean asks, incredulous.

"We're looking into it," Keith assures him.

I look back at Claire, who has gone silent again. She stands there, shaking, her eyes hollow. I lose all the fight in me at how defeated she looks. I slowly walk up to her, trying not to spook her, and cradle her cheeks.

"Come on. You're coming with me and Rye, and you will stay with us tonight, okay?" I say gently.

Claire's eyes shift to meet mine, and I get a singular nod in reply.

It's something.

***

Riley and I get Claire to our room, letting Andrea and Sean know that we will keep them updated throughout the night on how she is. Even though Keith and Theodore insisted that George was innocent, all I can see in my mind is him standing over Pru with the knife. My heart and head are conflicted with the information, and I can't stand to look at him right now.

We help Claire put on some of Riley's pajamas and tell her to make herself comfortable in bed. Once she lies down, we lie down on either side of her and wrap her up in our arms.

Claire breaks.

Not suddenly, not loudly, but slowly. It's like something inside her finally splinters.

She clings to us, sobbing so hard I feel it in my own chest.

***

We must have all dozed off after a while, because we all shot up in bed when there was a pounding at the cabin door.

"Lexi! Riley! Let me in!" A slurred voice comes from the other side

Riley and I share a look over Claire's head, and I hurry out of the bed to get to the door. I open it a crack.

"What the fuck do you want?" I hiss.

"I want to explain," George shouts, swaying.

The smell of alcohol seems like it's coming out of every one of his pores. He's more drunk than I have ever seen him.

I rush out into the hall, the door shutting behind me, and I slam George into the wall across from us. My arm goes to his neck, my forearm pressing lightly on it.

"You need to be anywhere but here." I look into his eyes, which are darting back and forth, trying to focus. "Go find somewhere to pass out."

His eyes meet mine, steady for a moment before they shift again. "I would never," he hiccups. "Hurt Pru," he whispers, the smell of whiskey washing over me.

I move my arm from his neck and cross my arms over my chest. "George," I sigh. "Go sober up and we'll talk in the morning."

He rubs his hands down his face. "I would never do that."

I stare at him, taking in his slumped shoulders and red-rimmed eyes. "I know." I lie.

I don't know, and I'm still not convinced, but anything to get him to walk the fuck away right now.

The door opens behind me, and Riley pokes her head out. "What in God's name... George." Her eyes narrow.

"I got it, Rye. George was leaving, and we'll talk to him in the morning." I don't break eye contact with the man.

George's eyes shine with tears, but he says nothing. He turns and walks away, shoulders hunched, footsteps unsteady, and for just a second, I wonder if I should hear him out.

I turn to Riley and kiss her. "I'm going to follow behind him and make sure he gets to his room."

Riley nods, and I grab my shoes from the doorway, throwing them on, and begin to follow the drunk man slowly.

CHAPTER
TWENTY-THREE

The ship was quiet, save for the distant groans of the hull against the waves, as it rocked through the storm that had finally reached them.

The man staggered down the hallway, one hand dragging along the wall to steady himself, the other fumbling with a half-empty glass.

Struggling to stay upright with every step, he cursed all the drinks he had consumed as the ship swayed from side to side. The overhead lights were bright and harsh, making him squint as he continued down the hallway.

He paused at the end of the hall, looking both ways, trying to remember his cabin number and direction.

"Goddammit," he murmured as he made a guess and veered to the right.

"Out late, aren't you?" A voice asked behind him.

He spun and almost fell at the quick movement. "What do you want?"

"Tsk Tsk," the newcomer clicked their tongue. "That's no way to speak to a friend."

"Friend?" He scoffed. "Get the fuck away from me."

He turned back around and continued his trek to find his room.

He could sense the other person behind him, but ignored the warning bells in his brain, blaming exhaustion and too many drinks.

"You're going the wrong way," the voice taunted.

A chill raced down his spine at the cold tone in the person's voice. "Fuck off!"

He began to doubt himself and paused, looking around him.

The other person needed that pause to come up behind him, one hand around his mouth and the other tight around his neck.

"Bad night to wander," the voice in his ear hissed.

The glass he had been holding shattered on the floor as his hands came up, clawing at the arm on his throat. He struggled to breathe as the arm tightened, stars forming before his vision.

He kicked his legs out, trying to hit the person, but it was useless. The grip didn't loosen.

They were more sober. Steadier.

They struggled to the end of the hall, and his eyes widened when he saw the staircase. He tried to shake his head, but he knew it wouldn't help him.

He was shoved over the railing.

Time slowed as the floor reached up to meet him, headfirst, in a twist of limbs.

CHAPTER TWENTY-FOUR

The next morning, we're woken up by the violent swaying of the ship. My stomach rolls with the sea, and I groan as I grip the edge of the mattress and slowly sit up.

"Make it stop," Riley whines, head buried in her pillow.

Claire sighs heavily as she sits up, running a hand through her hair before hiding her face in her hands.

Riley suddenly sits up, like she just remembered everything that happened, and wraps Claire up in a hug. Claire leans on her and sobs.

Riley looks at me over Claire's head, looking lost.

I clear my throat of the lump that has lodged itself there. "Let me see what Andrea and Sean are doing."

I lurch out of bed and grab my phone, steadying myself against the swaying floor as I reach the dresser.

I see that I have multiple missed messages from George:

Im sory - 1:30 AM

Please talk 2 me - 1:35 AM

I didn do anyhing. - 1:37 AM

I neeed yu - 1:45 AM

Somthng is goig on - 1:50 AM

Non of this is riht - 1:52 AM

Talk in the moring - 2:30 AM

"Jesus," I mutter as I read through the messages. My head spins. Anger rises first and then guilt.

Then something else, something that feels a hell of a lot like fear.

Riley appears behind me, peering at the messages over my shoulder. "What are we going to do about him?" she asks quietly.

"We should talk to him," I sigh and turn around to look at her. I notice Claire watching us from the bed, and I step away from Riley, not wanting to be too close in front of the broken woman.

"I think I need to shower," Claire says quietly, throwing her legs over the edge of the bed.

"You can shower here," Riley offers.

Claire nods once. "Thank you, but I need my things. I'm okay."

She gets up, finds her balance, and pauses halfway to the door, gripping the wall like the floor might give out beneath her. Then she turns, gives us each a fragile hug and a ghost of a smile, and disappears.

Riley turns to me and gives me a gentle kiss. "I'll be back soon. I'm going to go grab us some coffee."

"Please don't go alone," I whisper. "I don't think Claire should be going alone either."

Riley kisses me again. "We'll be fine." She cups my cheek, and I lean into it.

I watch her leave, and the feeling in my gut twists into something I can't name. I sit momentarily, trying to ground myself, then realize the feeling.

Foreboding.

***

Riley has been gone for about 10 minutes, and there is a knock on the cabin door.

"Already?" I mutter, expecting Andrea or Sean. But when I swing the door open, it's Keith and Theodore.

"Can't you two cut us a fucking break for a little?" I growl.

"You need to come with us, Lexi," Theodore says, voice even and a little cold.

"I'll find you later and finish my statement," I say.

"This isn't negotiable," Keith adds.

Riley appears next to the men. "It's eight in the morning. Can you two not come back later after we've had time to try to process anything?" She shoulders past them into the cabin.

Keith doesn't even glance at Riley. "Lexi, don't make this harder than it needs to be."

Riley looks between me and the two officers. "What the fuck is happening right now?"

I kiss her cheek, forcing a calm I don't feel. "I'll be back," I say, even though I have no fucking idea if that's true.

***

"Do I need to pay extra for how much time I spend in this fucking room?" I frown at the two men in front of me.

Keith and Theodore sit quietly, watching me. Neither of them has a hint of a smile, and it's unnerving how cold they both suddenly seem.

"Where were you last night?" Keith asks.

I can't help but scoff. "You mean before or after my friend died?" I tap my chin. "Or do you mean before or after you questioned me? Or *maybe* before or after you ambushed us with George without telling us what the fuck is going on?"

Something's off. The room's too quiet, their eyes too flat.

My stomach sinks just as the door creaks open behind me.

I expected another officer, or maybe just another round of questions. But the second I see Briggs, I know something's wrong.

"Alexandria Whitlock." Briggs says, his voice flat and cutting. "You are hereby being detained. You do have the right to remain silent."

My eyes widen, and suddenly, I realize this is not a joking matter.

"What the fuck?" I breathe.

Briggs slaps down a folder on the table and stands above me. "Where were you at approximately 2:00 in the morning?"

"I was sleeping," I blurt.

Even as I say it, I know how pathetic it sounds.

"Can anyone corroborate that?" Keith asks.

"Riley and Claire." I immediately answer. "What the fuck is happening right now?"

"A passenger found a body this morning," Theodore says, hands spreading out on the table.

"Another one?" I can't help but seethe.

"And we have surveillance of you roaming the area around this time."

Briggs flips open the folder. I catch a glimpse, and I'm already moving. The chair scrapes back, and I accidentally slam into Briggs, trying to get away from the image burned into my brain.

***

Walking back to the room, everything feels like it's spinning. The ship is rocking, and I'm barely holding it together as the hallways feel like they're closing in on me.

I make it to the cabin, eyes bleary, and I step in to see Riley and Claire sitting on the bed, and Andrea and Sean sitting on the couch.

Riley stands the second she sees me, eyes wide with concern. "Lex, what the fuck happened?" she asks.

I shake my head, and I can't speak.

My throat is dry. The words won't come out.

"Are you okay?" Sean asks. "What did they want with you?"

I cough, trying to steady myself. My hands are shaking, and I take a deep breath.

My voice comes out barely above a whisper.

"James is dead."

CHAPTER TWENTY-FIVE

Voices explode around me, all talking over each other. I can't make out a single question. It's overwhelming, and suddenly, I feel myself break into a cold sweat, and it starts getting hard to breathe.

"Guys," Riley's voice cuts through everyone else. "Guys, hold on." She comes and puts her hands on my cheeks. "Lex, breathe," she tells me.

I feel the walls closing in, and I break free from Riley to bend over and put my hands on my knees, trying to listen and breathe.

Someone's hands grip my arm, and suddenly I'm shoved through the balcony door, out into the storm.

The balcony door closing is muffled in my ears, and the roar of blood in my veins drowns everything else.

I know Riley is out here with me, but if she's talking to me, I don't hear it.

I try to ground myself. I focus on the sound of the waves against the ship. The smell of the salt in the wind. The pelts of rain on my face.

It starts to help, and I can finally stand upright. I see Riley leaning against the railing, looking out into the choppy water.

"Thank you," I gasp, finally able to breathe again. "You're welcome," she murmurs, still staring at the sea.

I wipe the water from my face with shaking hands.

James is dead. And they thought it was me.

They only let me go because I told them I followed George, and they found footage of me in his hallway when James went over the railing.

But of course, they wouldn't share a word about the rest of any footage.

Nothing makes any sense.

"Are you okay?" I ask Riley.

She turns to look at me and gives me a single nod. "You're the one who just had a panic attack. Are you okay?"

I take in a shaky breath. "I will be. Come on, let's go back in and I'll explain."

We go back into the cabin, and Andrea, Sean, and Claire look at us with concern.

Andrea stands up and comes to hug me. "You're okay," she reassures me softly.

"We need to get George," I say, bracing for the reaction.

Claire stiffens and stares at me. "I won't be in the same room as him."

"George didn't kill James. And I don't think he killed Pru either." I say.

I hold up my hand as everyone starts to talk.

"I followed him, and he went straight to his room after he left here." I pause, scanning their faces. "We need to stick together. Someone's targeting us."

***

George responds that he will meet us when I message him, and we decide to meet somewhere on the deck instead of cramming into a cabin. Claire sits rigid, trembling despite the oversized sunglasses hiding half her face, but they can't mask her jaw's wobble.

Andrea has been quiet, and Sean has a margarita in front of him. Riley and I sit, hands clasped, and we wait.

"Hey," George says quietly as he approaches us.

Sean gets up from his seat and walks up to him. They lock eyes for a moment before Sean grabs him in a hug. George's shoulders heave in relief as he hangs onto Sean tightly, and I can see some of the tension leave his body.

Once they break apart, George glances at Claire, who won't look at him. She stares straight ahead, her lips pressed into a line.

George lowers himself into a chair at the far end of the table and folds his hands together in his lap.

George looks at each of us, and his gaze lingers on Claire. "I know how things looked, and I don't blame you for thinking it was me. But I swear to you, I would never hurt anyone. Especially not Pru."

Claire doesn't move at first. Then, slowly, she turns her head toward him. "Tell me what happened."

George shifts in his seat. "I heard yelling, and I turned around. Pru was there," he clenches his jaw. "There was a knife. I should've left it, I know, but I was drunk. It didn't process. I thought if I pulled it out, she'd be okay. Like it hadn't happened."

A sob bubbles from Claire's throat.

Andrea leans over and intertwines her fingers with Claire's.

The silence thickens. No one knows how to respond.

Then Riley cuts in, voice quiet but sharp. "James is dead."

George's eyes go wide, and he starts shaking his head. "I didn't do it. I didn't kill anyone."

"We know," Sean says. "Lexi followed you last night to make sure you got to your room. We're not accusing you."

"Someone is trying to pit us against each other," Andrea says lowly, her eyes narrowing. "Someone is trying to break us apart and pick us off individually."

"We need to find them," I say. "And put an end to this."

"How do we do that?" Sean asks.

"We stick together. No one does anything alone, ever." I immediately respond. "Do not go off by yourself, keep your eyes open, and make sure you're aware of your surroundings."

"The buddy system," Claire pipes up. "Who is with whom?"

We all look around, knowing that even though George didn't kill Pru, Claire couldn't be paired with him. He was too close and involved for her to be comfortable with him.

"Claire, you and I can pair up." Sean puts a hand on Andrea's leg and squeezes.

"Rye, why don't you and Dre pair up?" I say, eyes flicking to George. "That'll leave me and George." Riley gives me a look like I've lost my mind, but nods. Someone needs step up, and Sean can't carry the whole burden of everyone's emotions and feelings right now. I know he's the only one besides me willing to pair with George, and even knowing he's innocent, that image of him with the knife still sticks in my mind.

"Now what?" Andrea asks.

"Now, we go back to where each death that we know of happened and look for security cameras in the area," I conclude. "I want to make sure that they actually reviewed the footage like they say they did."

Riley's eyebrow arches. "You don't trust them?"

I glance past the group, watching the unsuspecting people mill about, trying to enjoy their vacations amid the darkening storm.

"I don't trust anyone who isn't at this table."

And even then, that trust has been fractured and is hanging by a thread.

CHAPTER TWENTY-SIX

"I have to use the restroom," the young teen told his mother as she rocked his baby sister in her arms, ignoring him as she had throughout the cruise.

"Be quick," The mother chided. "You know that Eliza gets fussy if we sit too long."

He rolled his eyes, the action going unnoticed. "Yes, mother."

He got up from the table and wandered for a while, finding a bathroom out of the way to give himself a break from his baby sister and her constant screams. The "Out-of-Order" sign on the door only encouraged him, knowing that no one would come looking for him in this restroom.

He went to the empty stall and slumped down, heaving a sigh as he put his head in his hands.

He was promised a fun cruise with him and his mom, but then his deadbeat of a father said he wouldn't watch the baby, which meant she also had to come along. Instead of the promised fun trip, the teen had to put aside everything he wanted to do to cater to the baby.

Voices suddenly flooded the room, and the teen groaned to himself as two men started talking to each other.

So much for some time to myself.

One of the men entered the other open stall, all but one of the urinals taped off.

"How did you know?" The voice in the stall asked.

"Because I know you." The other voice said. "And I believe you."

The door creaked again as the teen heard the urinal flush and the sink come to life. Then he heard a shout and a dull thud.

Yanking up his feet on instinct, the boy began to tremble as he noticed a man who had fallen to the floor, blood pouring from a wound in his head.

The bathroom door opened next to him with a shout, and he watched as another man landed on the floor next to the first one.

Feet stood over both bodies, and the boy whimpered against his will, his knees shaking and his heart pounding in his ears.

The feet turned in his direction, and a knock sounded on the closed door.

"Come on out of there. I know you're in there." A voice sing-songed as the lock began to turn from the outside.

What good were locks on doors if someone could get in?

"Please, I didn't see anything, " the boy begged as the door flew open. His breath caught in his throat, and his mouth dried at the sight of the stranger.

The figure stood there and sighed heavily as they watched the boy put his hands up. "Well, now this won't do."

The boy was lifeless before he could even see what hit him.

CHAPTER
TWENTY-SEVEN

"Please stand by for an announcement from the Captain," the speakers blare, followed by three sharp chimes.

"Good morning, travelers. As you can tell, we're going through an intense storm. It's predicted to worsen, so as of this announcement, all activities on the outside decks have been canceled. All ongoing games have been cancelled. If possible, things will be moved inside. Please check with the nearest crew member for the most up-to-date information. Avoiding the outside decks while we navigate through the worst of it in the upcoming few hours is strongly suggested. We always strive to keep everyone safe while enjoying your time with us."

The announcement ends with three more chimes, and I can't help but roll my eyes.

"Safe," I scoff. "Yeah, sure. Until someone else turns up dead."

George is tense beside me, and I sigh.

"I don't blame you."

He stops next to me. "How can you not? I shouldn't have pulled out the knife."

I stop and pull him to the side of the hallway, getting out of the way of everyone walking past. "George... Pru was gone the second that knife hit her chest. None of us could've changed that."

I angrily wipe a tear away. Now is not the time.

"We all lost Pru, just like we all lost Hannah. There will be time to grieve, but right now we need to focus on survival and stopping anyone else from dying. We get through this cruise. That's what we focus on right now. After that, we figure it out. Together."

George stands up straighter and nods, blinking back his tears. "You're right."

"I'm always right," I joke, attempting to lighten the mood.

George smiles, but it doesn't reach his eyes. "Where to, fearless leader?"

"Dre and Rye are going to the dining area. Sean and Claire are going to the deck and the pool. You and I will check out the staircase where James died." I shiver. "Hopefully it's not still blocked off."

***

The staircase is still blocked off.

We poke around a corner to see security still combing the area.

"Back to the scene of the crime?" Theodore asks behind us, amused.

I startle and whirl around. "Theodore! Hello."

"What are you doing here?" he sighs heavily. "You shouldn't be here."

"Just out for a stroll," I reply, flashing him a grin that probably looks more like a grimace.

"If you get out of here right now, I won't tell anyone that you're poking around where the man you were accused of killing died." Theodore crosses his arms and leans against the wall.

George's eyes go wide, and I forget that he didn't hear the whole story of what happened.   He grabs my arm and pulls me back. "We're leaving."

Theodore watches us go, and once we're further away and around a corner, George yanks my arm to stop me.

"What the fuck was that about?"

I wince. "They might have accused me of killing James because I followed you back to your room last night, and they caught me on video roaming the halls."

"I meant to ask about that. You followed me?" George asks with a slight grin at the corner of his mouth.

"I got held up for murder, and you're more concerned that I followed you?" I scoff. "I wanted to make sure you were okay." I shrug.

George shakes his head. "Aren't we the Wonder Twins?"

I roll my eyes. "Come on, let's roam around for a while before we meet everyone else."

***

We meet everyone else at the designated time in a corner of the cafeteria. Since people are around every corner, we decided to brave the deck outside for more privacy. As the rain has gotten heavier, we take a covered table right outside.

The sky is dark, and the rain is hitting the deck loudly. The air has gotten cooler as the wind howls around us.

"You told me I wouldn't have to worry about Sharknado, and I'm starting to think you lied," Sean accuses me.

I can't help but throw my head back and laugh, caught off guard by the sense of normalcy I feel now. "If we see a Sharknado, I will forever be in your debt," I assure him.

"Did anyone get anything?" Andrea asks, bringing us back to reality.

George shakes his head. "Our area was still blocked off."

"We didn't see anything around the pool at first, but then we realized that the security camera in that area was facing the other direction. Same with the deck where you said that woman was found," Sean says.

"Dining room was normal," Riley shrugs. "Cameras in every direction, so they should have been able to see it. I think that was genuinely a heart attack."

I suddenly remembered the extra clue we had gotten. "Rye, do you remember where we put that clue at our cabin? We should compare it to the other clues, because I think it was purposefully left for us." I clear my throat. "It led us right to Hannah." I glance at George, and he looks down at his lap.

"I need to run to the bathroom," George says quietly, and I know he wants a moment alone.

"I'll go with you." Sean nods, and they stand up and go back inside.

"I don't believe security is being honest with us," I say to the rest of the table. "I think they are hiding something."

Claire watches the guys go inside, and her hands start to wring.

"It's not like they're going to be honest with us," Andrea says. "There's no reason for them to tell us anything."

"We've lost two people." Claire sighs. "You would think that they would listen when we tell them something is going on." She stands. "I need a drink."

Riley stands up as well. "I'm coming with you."

Claire holds her hand up. "Please. I'm going right inside. I will be fine. Just... give me a moment to myself. Please."

Riley frowns but sinks back into her chair as Claire disappears into the ship's halls.

Riley sits there for a while, looking out over the water, a contemplative look on her face.   We watch her, knowing she'll tell us what she thinks when ready. It only takes a moment more.

"Why does security keep coming for us when we're the ones dying?" She wonders.

We sit silently, letting those words sink in and get lost in our thoughts.

After a while, I check my watch and frown. "The guys have been gone for a while."

Andrea looks around, and she frowns as well. "Should we go check on them?"

"Maybe they're just catching up on things?" Claire suggests as she walks back up to the table with a drink.

That bad feeling that has been following me the entire cruise creeps back in. That sense that something isn't quite right.

I stand. "We need to find them."

The other girls follow me, and we stumble on a commotion down one of the far halls.

A crowd has gathered, shouting. My stomach turns to ice. Something is wrong.

Very wrong.

"Oh God." Andrea gasps as we start to run.

We wrestle our way through the people gathered outside the bathroom. The door has an "Out-of-Order" sign on it.

Sean is propped up against the wall right outside the door, his head resting against his chest. His eyes are closed, and he's covered in blood.

"Sean!" Andrea cries, shoving someone out of the way to kneel next to him. "Baby, no."

Sean opens his eyes and tries to focus on us. His eyes are glassy as he looks at Andrea.   There's a gash in his forehead bleeding freely.

A crew member arrives with a towel to press on the wound on his head, and he winces.

"George. Inside."

That's all Sean says, and we push into the bathroom.

The floor is slick and red. It smells like copper and bile in the small space. My foot hits it wrong, and I go sliding, Riley and Claire catching me just before I hit the tile. I grip onto Riley's arm as my eyes land on a body.

George lies crumpled on the floor, his head bleeding freely, matting his hair and painting the bathroom floor as his eyes try to focus.

"Oh fucking shit," Riley utters as she slowly walks through the blood to get to George.

She crouches down, checks for a pulse, and heaves a sigh in relief. "He's alive," she gasps in surprise.

"Guys..." Claire chokes out, and that's when I see it.

Legs under a bathroom stall, twisted and contorted like no person should ever be.

CHAPTER TWENTY-EIGHT

I clamp a hand over my mouth when I notice the person in the stall.

I trudge through the blood, every squelch under my shoes threatening to send bile up my throat, before I shove the door open.

It's a kid. Fifteen, maybe.

Who the hell is he, and why was he in here?

The wounds to his throat are extensive, and I can't even imagine the pain he went through.

"Oh my God," I dry heave and stagger back.

We shouldn't be here.

We are tracking blood everywhere. Ruining fucking evidence.

Goddammit.

"Get out," I cough, trying to prevent the vomit from coming up. "Get out *now*."

I push Riley and Claire toward the door, trying not to slip, but it's useless.

My foot slips on the slick tile and shoots out from under me, and I crash hard onto my back, staring up at a ceiling splattered with blood.

"Lexi!" Claire gasps and reaches for me, but a security officer hauls her back before she can.

"Let *go* of me!" Claire screams and thrashes.

"Ma'am, you're contaminating a scene," the officer barks as he pulls her backwards out of the door.

I just lay there. Cold, sticky blood clings to me, thick and jelly-like. It seeps through my clothes, and I cringe.

Keith comes into my vision, peering down at me.

"Why, in the *fucking* world," he mutters, "is it always *you*?"

I blink up at him. "Would you believe me if I said 'wrong place, wrong time'?"

"Get up," he snaps. "And get the hell out of my crime scene."

***

An officer escorts me back to our cabin and tells me to shower and change into new clothes quickly before we're all brought into the library once again. Everyone else is cleared out, and the doors shut behind the officer.

We all sit in uncomfortable silence as the ship rocks violently. The lights flicker, and my nausea returns.

"We were told none of you would talk if separated, so we're doing this together." The officer begins, and I raise a brow. "So, tell me what happened—from the beginning."

Sean sits slumped in a new outfit, butterfly bandages on his forehead, an ice pack pressed to the swelling. "George and I went to the bathroom. All of a sudden, I'm knocked out, and the next thing I know, George is on the floor, not moving."

"Where were you when you were knocked out?" The officer asks, flipping open his notebook.

"Officer..." Riley squints at his nameplate. "What's your name?"

"Smith," he grunts.

"Officer Smith," she tries to smile, but it falls flat. "We've had a hell of a week. Sean just got his head bashed in, and George is in the medical bay. Do we really need to do this?"

Officer Smith glares at Riley until she huffs and crosses her arms over her chest. He then turns back to Sean.

"Go ahead." It's an order, not a question.

Sean winces as he moves the ice pack. "I was standing at the sink washing my hands, and I turned around to grab the paper towels and got hit with something."

"Did you see anyone enter the bathroom?" Officer Smith writes down Sean's answer. "Why were you in a bathroom that was out of order?"

"Not at all. And we figured it would give us some privacy to talk without many people coming in. We found the furthest bathroom possible and decided to ignore the sign."

The officer glares at Sean. "Was the person already in the bathroom with you?"

"Did you not hear him?" Andrea snaps. "He has no idea what happened."

Officer Smith sighs and closes his notebook. "Look, we're trying to determine what happened to you and your friend. Anything you can give us will help us find who did this."

Sean nods. "Honestly, sir, I didn't see anything. I came to, and George was lying on the floor. I thought he was dead." He chokes on the words. "I crawled into the hall, and people started screaming."

Sean is talking, Andrea is snapping, and all I can think about is that kid who got caught up in whatever the fuck is going on.

"I've been instructed to tell you to go to the Main Theatre and not move. You've been ordered to stay there for the day, where people can watch you." Officer Smith stands. "We will lock you up for the rest of the cruise if we find you anywhere but that room."

"What about food? And having to go to the bathroom?" Claire presses defiantly.

"Food will be brought to you, and you can get a security escort to the restroom. There will be four of us stationed in the room with everyone," he explains. "Now, let's go."

We file out of the room and head for the Main Theatre. The sky outside is dark, even though it is ten o'clock in the morning. As we are walking, we hear a scream, and my entire body seizes in fear. The screaming doesn't stop, and I realize it's not terror.

It's heartache.

The kid's mother. Those screams are of an indescribable loss.

My anger flares, and my body shakes with rage.

No mother should have to see her kid carved up like that. No one should have to bury what's left of their child.

***

We're in the back of the Main Theatre, seething with the almost loss of more friends and the actual loss of another innocent teenager.

There's no more time for grief. Not when we're being hunted.

All I can think about is that poor child in the bathroom, and now we have to sit here watching a goddamn magic show.

It's not right, and it makes every nerve in my body light up with anger.

The lights flicker every time we hit a wave, and scared kids surround us, ratcheting the tension. The crew member running the show is trying to keep everyone calm, but it's damn near impossible with the parents so strung out.

I scan the room and clock only three security officers: Theodore, Smith, and another guy I've seen before—hair clipped close, built like a linebacker, always silent. They circle like sharks, observing everyone and occasionally murmuring into their radios.

One kid won't stop screaming, and his parents are clearly overwhelmed. I watch Theodore approach, crouch to the kid's level, and show him his open palms.

Then, he swipes behind the kid's ear and "finds" a coin, eyes wide like it's magic.

The child quiets. Smiles.

Theodore hands him the coin with a wink, then pulls a sticker from his pocket. He ruffles the kid's hair before standing and moving on to the next restless child.

"We need to find a way to get out of here," Riley says lowly. "I cannot be trapped here like this, or I will go crazy."

Andrea balks. "Did you not hear when they said that we are being watched and will be locked up if we leave?"

"Maybe that's the safest thing for us," Claire says. "If we're locked up, no one can come for us. No one else will die."

"Yeah, I don't think that's necessarily true," Andrea sighs.

Sean sits with his eyes closed, and I can tell he's in a world of pain.

Physically and emotionally.

"Sean, are you okay?" I ask gently.

Sean cracks his eyes open and takes a moment to focus on me. "I'm feeling pretty sick."

I turn and flag down one of the officers. Smith approaches with trepidation written on his face.

"Yeah, hi," I start. "Is there anything you can get Sean here for his nausea? He has a pretty gnarly head wound, and they didn't do much for him."

The officer studies Sean, who grimaces at him. He sighs and speaks into his portable. "Can I get a medic to the Main Theatre?"

I sigh in relief that someone is actually listening to us for a change. This is progress.

We only have to wait about 10 minutes before a medic appears. He kneels in front of Sean and moves his bangs out of the way so that he can examine the wound. He winces, and I notice how badly the area has begun to bruise. Security shuffles around us as we watch the man attend to Sean.

Suddenly, the lights go out and we're thrown into utter darkness.

Children scream while parents yell.

The ship rocks violently from side to side.

I panic and reach for Riley's hand, and find hers reaching for mine

"Is everyone okay?" I ask into the blackness.

"Good." Andrea breathes out, her voice coming in gasps.

"I'm here," Claire says into the blackness.

I feel something sharp on my arm, and I wince.

What the fuck?

The lights return in what feels like a lifetime later, and we all look around, expecting the worst.

CHAPTER TWENTY-NINE

Once my eyes have focused, I realize that Officer Smith is on the ground, clutching his stomach, a dark red seeping out from between his fingers. The medic has been shoved onto the floor as well and scrambles to his side.

"I need some help here!" He screams as he puts pressure on the officer's hands on his stomach. Theodore comes running over.

"Fucking shit." Riley's voice shakes. Her eyes are wide and terrified.

I look down and realize my arm is bleeding from a gash in my forearm. "What the fuck happened?" I gasp and clamp my other hand down on it.

"Guys," Sean says slowly.

"Babe!" Riley gasps. "What the hell?"

"Oh my God, is he gonna-" Claire's voice cracks, eyes locked on the officer's stomach.

"Guys," Sean says again, his voice too soft and calm. We turn. Blood is everywhere.

"Sean!" Andrea gasps, dropping to her knees. Her hands go to the blood soaking through his pants. "Fuck! What happened?"

Sean's face glistens with sweat. "I think I got stabbed." He looks down at his leg and the growing pool under him.

Time shatters, and I can't breathe.

I stare at Sean's leg.

He looks up at me. Our eyes lock. I see the resignation.

"Take care of her." He coughs again.

No.

I launch forward. "Don't you fucking dare." I slam my hand down on his leg, putting as much pressure as I can, ignoring my own wound. "Theodore!" I scream.

Theodore jolts up from beside the injured officer, eyes wide when he sees Sean and bolts toward us.

"Did you get injured?" He asks Sean, who is becoming paler and paler by the moment.

Sean only nods.

"We need more medics. Now!" Theodore barks into his radio, then drops beside me, his hand covering mine, pressing harder.

Riley's taken his spot by the officer, helping the medic. She's covered in blood from hand to elbow, and my stomach rolls at the sight.

Keith has also appeared out of nowhere and helps them.

I glance at Claire and nod toward Andrea. "Do you have her?"

Claire wraps her arms around Andrea, who is sobbing, reaching out for Sean.

Theodore rips off his belt and cinches it around Sean's thigh.

Sean screams and gasps for air as Theodore pulls it as tight as he can. I know it's too late.

The wound is too far up on his thigh for it to be effective.

"Dre..." Sean chokes. "Andrea, I love you so much."

Andrea wails. "Please don't do this."

It's as if time stops. He reaches for her face with a trembling hand and pulls her in. Their lips meet, shaking and desperate.

One last kiss.

Their goodbye.

***

It doesn't take long for Sean to pass out from the blood loss.

The medics evaluated Sean and advised that his femoral artery was hit. They used all their resources, a junctional device and direct pressure, but without surgery, there was nothing they could do that would save him. It was useless - the blood was unstoppable.

The storm made getting a chopper in time to med-vac him out impossible.

We watched as the life left his body, an agonizing ten minutes after the lights came back on.

Andrea and Claire huddle together in the corner. Riley and I stand side by side, watching the medics still working on Smith.

Another medic had looked at my arm and patched up the shallow wound, advising that I might need stitches. I ignored him and waved him off.

Riley grips my hand tightly as some officers cover Sean's body.

"Lex," she whispers. "I can't do this. I can't lose anyone else."

She's looking at me like I can fix this. But I can't.

Not this time.

There's a spattering of red on her chin where she must've wiped her face with a bloody hand. I lift the hem of my shirt and wipe it away.

"No one else is dying today," I tell her.

But even as I say it, I know the truth.

I have no control right now, and we need to get it back.

"Come on. We're going to our room," I say, adrenaline pumping through my veins as I pull her with me as we head toward Andrea and Claire.

"Let's go," I tell them. "We're done playing this game."

Andrea is still sobbing as Claire hoists her to her feet. The four of us push through the dazed crowd and slip out the doors.

***

Hannah.

Pru.

Sean.

Our friends are dead. Our loved ones are dead.

We make it to our cabin and collapse into silence. The storm outside has only worsened. The wind howls against the windows, rain pelting the glass.

We're all dirty and exhausted and lost in our own thoughts.

Andrea and Claire have curled up on the bed, both silently crying. I stand near the window, looking out into the storm.

Riley comes behind me and rests her chin on my shoulder, arms around my waist.

"I love you," she murmurs.

We stare out into the dark, endless water. The waves rise higher with every passing minute.

"I want to find whoever's doing this and make them fucking pay," Andrea says from the bed.

She sits up, eyes lit with something raw.

Rage.

She stands. "I'm not locking myself in this room while some psycho walks free."

"It's the safest thing we can do," Riley mutters, voice flat.

I watch Andrea start pacing, her fists clenched tight. She's made up her mind. I know that look.

We're blood.

"What are you thinking?" I ask.

Riley and Claire both whip their heads toward me.

Andrea looks between us. "We draw them out. And then we stop them."

I step up beside her. "How?"

Claire jumps to her feet, disbelief all over her face. "Have you completely lost it? You want to *invite* this maniac to kill us?"

Riley sinks onto the bed, defeated. "You think they're gonna listen to reason right now?" She asks Claire.

"You're going to get us killed," Claire scoffs, arms crossed.

"Then stay here," Andrea snaps. "See how long that keeps you safe."

Claire flinches. Her voice trembles. "Who else has to die before this cruise is over? Every time I turn around, there's another body. I can't do this anymore."

I look her in the eye.

"All of us will die if we don't fight back."

Claire scoffs. "So, what do you propose then? Throw on a sparkly top and stand in the middle of the Atrium?"

Andrea lifts a brow. "Not a bad idea."

Claire throws up her hands and drops back onto the bed beside Riley.

"No, listen," Andrea says, more serious now. "We use one of us as bait. The others watch from a distance."

Riley makes a face. "Dre, that never works in the movies."

"This isn't a movie, it's survival." I cut in. "We're being hunted. We need to draw them out. On *our* terms."

Riley glares at me. "And who's going to be the bait?"

"They took Sean from me," Andrea chokes on a sob. "I'm the bait."

CHAPTER THIRTY

Our plan had Andrea stationed in the Atrium in one of Riley's sparkly shirts, planted at the bar, pretending to pound back drinks until it was convincing enough that she was drunk. The rest of us were positioned at different vantage points with visualization to watch.

I was out on the deck, watching through the window. Riley was hidden in the office near guest services. Claire was hanging out on the upper level overlooking the Atrium.

The goal was simple: monitor from every angle and wait to see if anyone took the bait.

We'd been at it for about an hour. I can't stay still. Restless energy claws at me.

George messaged us that he had been released from the medical bay and instructed to return to his cabin. We didn't tell him our plan, knowing he would want to help but be too injured to do any good.

None of us mentioned that we had lost Sean.

A man saunters up to Andrea, and my heart jumps into my throat.

Finally.

I press my face to the glass for a clearer view.

She sways on her barstool, acting drunk even though she has only been drinking mocktails. She barely gives the stranger the time of day, and I can see the man's jaw tighten.

I move inside the door, careful to stay hidden in the shadows so that I can listen.

"Come on, we can go somewhere a little quieter," he says, his voice oozing charm that doesn't reach his eyes.

Andrea hiccups. "No, thank you."

My stomach turns. I know she's acting, but he doesn't.

And he's way too close.

She's convincing. Too convincing.

And he's not backing off.

I tense, every muscle coiled. It takes everything I've got so as not to blow the plan.

The man scoots closer. "I can get you another drink with a little umbrella."

Andrea sways again, playing up the part, but her fingers clench the edge of the bar a second too tightly.

"You're cute." She slurs with a goofy smile.

He lights up. "I've got a private room. No screaming kids, no nosy crew." He stands.

Andrea stands as well, too fast.

My breath catches.

Is she pulling the plug? Did he scare her?

But then she wobbles, gives him another dopey grin, and slurs, "Lead the way, Captain."

I look up and make eye contact with Claire, who nods at me. I search for Riley and see that she has snuck out of the office and is watching from behind a fake tree, hidden from his view.

The guy grabs Andrea by the elbow and begins to lead her away. I see Claire hustle down the stairs behind them, and Riley pops out from behind the tree as I watch.

Once they reach the elevator, we close in.

We make it before the doors shut and step inside.

He doesn't even look at us. He leans in to whisper something to Andrea. She flinches and meets my eyes.

My pulse pounds in my veins.

The elevator dings, and he pulls her into the dim hallway beyond.

The three of us quietly follow behind them, ready for anything.

The air is thick with tension, and I can see Andrea trying to pull her arm away from him, but his grip tightens.

Andrea moves like lightning.

One second, he's smug, the next, he's pinned to the wall and screaming.

"Got you, fucker." She snarls.

The man's eyes go wide, and he cries out in pain. "What the fuck is wrong with you, you crazy bitch."

"Me?" Andrea scoffs.

We rush to them, and I push Andrea out of the way to spin him around and slam his back against the wall.

"Let's get security." I grit out and stare at the bewildered man in front of me.

"Security?" He panics. "I was just trying to get some action!"

"Action?" Riley crosses her arms over her chest. "Is that what you call murdering all of our friends?"

"I'm the fastest. I'll go get them," Claire announces and runs toward the elevator.

The man's eyes go so wide they almost roll out of his head. "Murder?" He squeaks and trembles under my hands.

Andrea slaps him hard across the face.

"Dre!" I admonish.

He whimpers, then freezes.

He looks down, and I follow his gaze.

No. No fucking way.

A wet stain spreads across his leg.

"Guys..." I mutter, the weight of it slamming into me. "It's not him."

"What?" Riley hisses, eyes darting around the dark hallway.

"He's not our guy." I shove away from him.

He scurries away from me and bolts down the hallway.

Andrea looks like a rabid animal. "Goddammit, Lexi. Why did you let him go?" She makes a move to chase him.

I grab her arm, yanking her back. "Dre, stop. It's not him." I try to make eye contact. "Look at me!"

She stops fighting me long enough to look at me, her eyes welling with tears.

"It wasn't him. He was terrified of us." I explain.

"Yeah, cause he's faking it!" Riley snaps.

"No," I shake my head. "I feel it in my gut, it's not him."

Andrea turns and punches the wall and then slides down it, crying.

Riley kneels next to her and pulls her into her arms.

My chest tightens. "Shit. Claire."

I'm already running before either of them can react.

***

Claire's gone. There's no sign of her anywhere.

By the time Andrea and Riley catch up to me at guest services, I've already grilled the front desk. No one has come by, and no one has asked for security.

"She didn't come here?" Andrea's voice cracks.

"No. Nothing."

I want to check the brig, but it's locked down, and there is no way to get there. No way Claire could've gotten in there on her own.

"Let's split up and look for her," Riley offers.

I'm already shaking my head. "No fucking way. We stay together."

"Lex is right," Andrea says quickly.

Riley exhales hard, frustration bleeding into panic. "Why the hell did we think we could find this asshole on our own?"

I glance at my watch. It's five. Still early, but the storm hasn't eased. It pounds against the ship like it's trying to rip it apart.

"Where would she go?" I mutter, mostly to myself.

Andrea shifts anxiously. "Should we check your room?"

Riley nods. "Let's go. Now."

***

We run to our room, and it's empty.

I grab a pillow off the bed and scream into it, my frustration bubbling over.

"There are so many places she could have gone." Andrea sighs, exhaustion starting to show on her face.

Our phones suddenly beep, and Riley jumps and puts a hand to her heart.

It's Claire.

Meet me in my room.

We all look at each other and rush off.

***

We reach the room, and I pound on the door, the sound matching the thunder outside.

Claire opens the door, white as a sheet, and beckons us in.

"Where the fuck did you go? Why didn't you go get security?" Andrea growls.

"A woman stopped me in the hall and handed me this." Claire shakily hands me a piece of paper.

Now is the time you must heed,

And here's one more clue you need.

Keep looking until the water bleeds.

"What?" I whisper, trying to understand. "I'm not good at this. I haven't found any clues.   What does this even mean?"

Riley grabs the paper from me and reads it. "I thought that all of the games were over." She looks up at Claire. "Who gave this to you?" She demands.

Claire shrugs. "A woman stopped me as I was walking to guest services. She was in a crew uniform and just handed it to me. She didn't even say anything, just shoved it at me and walked away."

"Why didn't you call security?" Andrea wonders.

Claire rounds on her. "For what? Some guy who pissed his pants?"

We all stop and stare at her.

"You ran off before he did that. How do you know that?" I stand up and begin to pace.

Something isn't right.

Claire looks embarrassed, and she looks at us. "I got scared to go alone and stopped at the end of the hall to see what happened. I saw everything. I figured there was no reason to alert anyone after you let him go, so I started to walk back to you guys, but stopped."

"What, and then you decided it was safe to leave alone?" Riley asks, skeptical.

"I figured alerting security about a man taking advantage of women was just as important, so I decided to go get them anyway," Claire shoots a nasty look at Riley.

I sigh. "What's done is done. We need to figure out this clue."

Andrea grabs it from Riley and stares at it for a while. "Until the water bleeds..." She looks thoughtful. "What always has water?"

Riley's eyes light up. "The pools!"

***

We rush out into the storm, bracing ourselves against the elements. All I can hear is the rain smacking against the deck, and I'm already soaked through from the wind-driven rain.

"Where do we even start?" Riley wonders and cowers when a shot of thunder rolls through the sky.

"The Lido Deck has multiple pools," Claire says.

I nod and we're off.

We make it to the pools, dread churning in my gut.

There's nothing there in any of the pools.

I turn to look at the other girls, and my frustration mounts. "There's nothing fucking here."

"Could they mean the rain?" Andrea looks up at the pouring rain.

Riley shakes her head. "What about hot tubs?"

I stare at her. "There are a million fucking hot tubs on this ship." I throw my arms out. "How the hell do we narrow it down?"

"Deck by deck." Andrea nods at Riley.

We start our trek along the sides of the Lido deck and find nothing in any of the hot tubs.

"What about the adults-only section?" Claire suggests hesitantly.

A shiver runs through me, and I look at Riley, knowing we're both thinking about Hannah.

"It makes sense. It's more private, and fewer people will brave the storm up there." Andrea says.

We all look at each other momentarily, then hurry to the upper deck.

Before I even make it to the top of the stairs, I can see the hot tub at the top of the deck.

I hold my breath as we take the last few stairs, and then I fall to my knees when the hot tub fully comes into view.

It's filled with red water sloshing over the sides. A hand is hanging over one side, and I don't need to look to know what I will see.

George is floating inside.

"Son of a bitch!" Andrea cries out and puts her hands to her face.

Riley takes a stop closer and sees the marks along his arms.

He's been murdered the same way as Hannah, with his wrists slit.

CHAPTER THIRTY-ONE

We find ourselves in the same position we have been most of the cruise, surrounded by security. Andrea had rushed to guest services, and now security swarms us everywhere.

There are plainclothes officers I've never seen before—probably hiding in plain sight this entire cruise—and all the uniformed ones I've had run-ins with, including Briggs and Keith.

"How did you know to come up here?" Briggs asks me, his face stony and his eyes hard.

I gulp. If he's here too, then maybe they finally believe me.

"There was a clue. We were playing the murder-mystery game, and a crew member gave Claire a piece of paper with a clue."

I look around to have Claire add to the story and sigh heavily.

Claire's gone. There's no sign of her anywhere.

Why the fuck would she run off in the middle of this?

I pull my phone out and message her.

Where the fuck did you go? - Me

"I honestly don't know what happened to George." I plead. "Can I please go look for Claire. I don't like any of us being alone now that half of us are dead." I can't help but spit the words with anger.

I went to find the woman who gave me the paper. I'm trying to find out who gave it to her. - Claire

Where are you? - Me

I'll let you know when I find her. - Claire

I feel heartless leaving George, as if he means nothing, but now, finding Claire, who is still alive, is more important.

"Let's split up and look for her," Riley offers.

I'm already shaking my head. "No fucking way. We stay together."

"Lex is right," Andrea says quickly. "We don't split up anymore. Every time we've gone against it, one of us dies."

I glance at my watch. It's five. Still early, but the storm hasn't eased. It pounds against the ship like it's trying to rip it apart.

"Where would she go to look for this woman? " I mutter, mostly to myself.

"Should we check near guest services?" Andrea suggests.

I nod. "That's a good idea."

We watch as the officers are distracted and slowly sneak away to find Claire.

***

We make the trek to guest services and don't see Claire anywhere on the way or at the desk.

The woman behind the desk glares at us as we approach, her hand reaching down for her panic button. We don't stop to talk to her, and I see her sigh in relief.

"Guys, I don't think she's here." Riley groans in frustration.

"Why would she leave like that? We were probably safer there than anywhere else on this ship." Andrea ponders.

Meet in the gym - Claire

"What the fuck?" Riley mutters at Claire's message. "Why would she be in the gym?"

We sprint down the corridor, rounding a corner to reach the outer deck leading toward the gym. Rain lashes sideways, and the storm is still merciless.

Just as I reach for the next door, a hand clamps on my arm.

"Wait." Riley's voice is low, tense. "This doesn't feel right."

I turn. Her eyes are locked on the rain-soaked path ahead.

"Why would she come out here?"

Andrea wipes water from her face, breathless. "What choice do we have, Rye?"

Riley shakes her head slowly. "No, think about it. The gym? While the storm's still going?"

"You think Claire's involved?" I ask, brow furrowed.

I finally voice what has been eating at me.

That one of us may be in on this.

Andrea's face twists. "Are you serious? Pru's dead. Claire was wrecked."

"Think about it. Really think about it. How could one person be doing this? Why are we the targets? How would all of our personal information get out..." I fold my arms tight across my chest, voice unsteady. "I agree with Rye. Something's *off*. Maybe she's working with someone."

Andrea and Riley share a glance, and Riley nods. "Okay, babe. We'll be careful, okay?"

I bite my lip in thought, not wanting to fall for a trap.

But then I nod.

***

We slow our pace as we approach the gym. It's dark inside, and there is a sign on the door saying the gym is closed. Given the weather around us, this makes sense.

I take a deep breath, the chill in the air making my lungs burn, and I push open the door.

It's dead quiet and pitch black.

"Claire?" My voice trembles as it echoes in the room.

No reply.

I hear a drip, assuming the water is getting in from the ceiling.

I slide my hand along the wall, looking for the light switch.

I flip the switch and let out a scream.

Claire hangs from the cable rack, arms bound above her by resistance bands.

Her stomach is slit open from end to end. Blood pools beneath her, thick and glossy.

Her head lolls toward her sternum at an angle that's wrong. The sound I thought was water is blood dripping.

"Son of a *bitch*!" I yell, slamming my palm against the wall.

"No, no, no." Andrea cries, folding in on herself, knees hitting the floor.

Riley doesn't move. Just stares. Her fists clench at her sides. When she finally turns to us, her eyes are blazing.

"This ends. Now." She turns and walks out the door.

Andrea takes one last look at Claire and follows Riley out of the gym.

I can't peel my eyes away from Claire. The guilt I feel even suspecting her makes my eyes fill with tears. I can hear her laugh in my head, and it's a cold contrast to what I see now.

***

We stumble back to our room and change out of our soaked clothes, too numb to care how cold we are.

Another of us.

Lost.

Dead.

It's six. Dinner's being served somewhere, but none of us is hungry. I haven't eaten all day, but the thought of food makes me sick.

"What now?" Andrea asks, and I cringe at the hopelessness in her voice.

I sit on the edge of the bed, soaked to the bone and shaking from more than the cold.

Riley stares out the window like she's trying to see through the storm. Andrea hasn't moved from the floor.

I close my eyes.

"I have an idea, but you won't like it."

Andrea and Riley share a withering look, knowing that things are about to get worse before they can get better.

CHAPTER THIRTY-TWO

The ship sways hard beneath me, the storm dragging the approaching night down with it. I recheck my phone to see if Andrea has messaged me. I have no new notifications, and the knot in my stomach tightens.

"Come on, Andrea. Answer me." I mutter as I attempt to get to the dining room, gripping the railing and fighting for balance. I took the outside walkway to avoid the crush of bodies inside, all of them doing their best to dodge the rain.

I guess people finally took what the Captain said about being outside to heart, because I haven't passed a soul.

"Lexi." A voice calls out behind me as I turn a corner, making me jump and whirl around.

"Keith!" My hand flies to my chest. My heart's pounding. "Jesus, you scared me." There is no one else in sight. "What are you doing out here?"

"I was looking for you," he nervously looks around. "I need to talk to you."

My eyes are drawn to Keith's hands as they hover near his waist, and warily, I watch as they twitch. "What about?"

"I know you know something strange is going on. I know you've pieced it all together." He takes a deep breath.

"Keith..." I glance behind me and take a step back, but I don't have anywhere else to go as my back hits the railing.

Keith takes a step forward, closing the gap I tried to create. His hands are extended in front of him. "I need your help."

"Why me?" I gulp.

"There you are!" Theodore suddenly bursts from one of the starboard doors onto the deck.   I'm still stuck against the railing, with Keith now in between us.

"I've been looking for you, Keith."

Keith pales, his eyes terrified as they meet mine. "Run."

I freeze, looking between the men. "What the fuck is going on?"

This wasn't part of the plan.

Fuck.

Keith reaches down to his waistband and retrieves a taser. "Theodore, we can figure this out." The weapon stays at his side as he stares his partner down, using his body to block mine,

My eyes don't leave the weapon as my heart rate quickens.

"Figure it out? I already did that." Theodore nods his head towards the taser. "And I think you know that I figured it out." He reaches toward his waistband and pulls out a gun.

How the fuck did he get a gun on a cruise ship?

Keith points the taser at Theodore, and a cold wave of fear washes over me. "Oh fuck..." I whisper. "Keith, no," I say loud enough for him to hear me.

"It's not what you think!" Keith screams, looking wildly around, still positioned between me and Theodore.

He looks like a trapped animal.

"It's exactly what you think." Theodore snarls and puts his hands up. "Lexi, I found Keith's room full of pictures of the crime scenes. It looked like a fucking episode of Criminal Minds in there. He has pictures of your whole group up there and the others. I think he's targeting you." He takes a slow step towards the other man.

I watch as tears form in Keith's eyes, and my heart sinks to my feet. "Jesus Christ." I start to shift away again, keeping my eyes trained on him. "You fucking killed them?"

"I didn't do it!" Keith cries out, his finger moving over the trigger of the taser still pointed at Theodore. Snot drips from his nose, and he wipes it on his sleeve. "I have no idea what he's talking about!"

Theodore keeps one hand out in peace while he indicates his shirt pocket. Keith nods once, and Theodore reaches inside. "Look," he pulls out what looks like photographs. "I brought the proof with me." He holds them out to me. "See for yourself." He keeps eye contact with Keith as he sets the photos on the deck, fans them out, and backs up.

The rain hasn't let up. If anything, it pours harder, and the papers on the floor begin to soak through and slosh back and forth in the water accumulated on the deck.

The ship keeps swaying, and the entire situation has me feeling dizzy.

"Keith, put it down," I beg the man.

I watch as he tenses up, eyes glancing at me and then training back on Theodore.

"I can't do that, Lexi," Keith sobs. "I am so sorry."

A door slams behind us, and then all hell breaks loose. My arm erupts in an explosion of pain. I fall to my knees with a choked scream, clutching the place where it hurts the most, disoriented and drowning in agony. I curl up, hands over my head, wanting to vanish from whatever is happening.

My ears are ringing, but I hear the muffled sound of shouting and loud pops, and I see the sky light up with the muzzle flashes.

I look through my hands and see that Keith has fallen to the deck, the blood already soaking the ground beneath him. Theodore is kneeling on one knee, holding his chest. The taser that has fallen from Keith's hand arcs uselessly in the rain.

He stands and pulls the prongs from his shirt, uninjured by what is sure to be a vest worn under it.

Theodore keeps his gun trained on Keith's unmoving form.

"Lexi," Theodore shouts. "Get away from him!" He stands and begins to walk towards the fallen officer.

A searing pain blooms down my arm from my bicep. I stagger back, clutching it. My hand comes away soaked in red.

Blood.

Bile rises in my throat.

"I'm shot?" I gasp, dazed.

I'm confused and have no idea what happened. Everything was a blur, and my mind won't let me pinpoint anything. All I can hear is the rain pelting the deck and the dull hum of gunshots in my ears.

Somewhere, the PA system blares out something unintelligible intermittently.

"Alexandria, come here now," Theodore growls. "We have to get you to Andrea and Riley."

I feel like I've been sucker punched.

His whole posture has changed.

He stands tall, towering over Keith, who still hasn't moved.

"Oh my God," I whisper as it hits me. I see the bullet hole in Keith's head, the blood still pouring, and being washed by the rain under the railing. "No, no, *no*."

"I was protecting you," Theodore says, too calm. "He was going to kill you. All of you." He puts his gun away and kicks Keith's discarded taser under the banister and into the dark water below.

"After the first mysterious death, the Staff Captain signed out one firearm to be on the safe side. Having a background in law enforcement, they let me hold onto it."

I look into his eyes and see nothing.

There is nothing behind them.

I watch in horror as he bends down and places his arms under Keith's shoulders to hoist him into a sitting position. With a grunt, he drags him, a trail of blood following, as he opens a stairwell door and tosses him carelessly inside.

"Are we going to get help?" I ask meekly.

I know we're not, but shock is a hell of a thing. Theodore just raises and amused brow at me.

"You fucking bastard!" I shout. "It's you! It's been you all along!" I look around wildly.

He wipes his hands on his pants and stretches his back. "You really thought *he* pulled this off?" He chuckles, low and bitter. "You ruined it, Lexi. The ending. The buildup. All of it." He clicks his tongue. "What a goddamn waste."

I stand up straighter, ignoring the pain as I look him dead in the eye. "How..." I snarl. "How did you pull it off?"

"It wasn't hard, if that's what you're wondering." He laughs, and the sound sends shivers down my spine. "At first, it was random. But then you and your little friends kept popping up everywhere." He shrugs and takes a step closer to me. "You should know you made yourselves very easy targets."

"Why us?" I grit out, my eyes trying to focus through the pain.

"Why not?" Theodore shrugs. "There's no rhyme or reason to it. I did it because I wanted to."

"How did you not get caught?" I wonder.

"I'm one of the security leads. I know where the cameras are and where they aren't. Erasing and looping footage isn't hard." He sighs as if he's bored. "If you're looking for some big motive why I kill people, you're going to be disappointed." He steps right up to me. "I do it because I'm bored. Because I can. And because it's fun."

The PA system is still crackling in the background, and Theodore smiles. "Looks like the PA system isn't exactly working as it should be either." He grins wickedly.

"Are you going to kill me now, too?" I ask. My chin is lifted in defiance.

I'm terrified.

But I won't show it.

"Lexi!" Riley's voice tears through the storm as she appears behind him from one of the side doors.

"Rye, no!" I scream.

What the fuck is she doing?

"This is exciting!" Theodore booms, spinning and pulling his gun again, training it on her. "A two-for-one!" His grin stretches across his whole face. "I guess technically a *three*-for-one if you count poor Keith."

Riley's eyes widen.

"The Coast Guard is on their way!" I shout, my eyes never leaving hers.

He laughs. "No, they're not. It's such a shame that the VHF radio went down." He flashes a smirk. "Those damn malfunctioning cameras made it pretty easy to destroy things."

He glances up at the sky. "Besides, they'll never make it in this storm. The comms are all down now."

He moves his finger to the trigger. "Where's the other one? Your sister."

"I don't know!" I cry. "Please, don't. I'll do whatever you want."

Theodore raises a brow. "Where's the fun in that?" He looks at Riley and then looks back at me. "You two are close, right?"

He pulls the trigger.

My whole world stops.

Riley flies backward and crumples to the deck, grasping her chest with a gasp.

The storm howls around us, thunder rumbling in the distance.

I'm rooted in place, staring at where Riley fell.

She isn't moving.

She's lying on her side, facing away, and I can't tell if she's breathing.

Blood from my arm drips down my fingers, splattering against the deck in fat red drops.

"You fucking psycho!" I scream, rain and tears mixing on my face. "I swear to *God*, I will fucking kill you."

Theodore rolls his eyes like I'm an inconvenience. "I'd like to see you try." He holsters his gun and strides toward me.

His hand lashes out and clamps around my throat.

"Let go," I rasp, barely audible, as I claw at his hand.

He tilts his head, studying me with disturbing curiosity. "You're tough. I'll give you that." His grip tightens.

Black spots speckle my vision.

"Too bad you weren't tough enough to save them all." His tone is mockingly tired, like he's bored.

I drive my knee up hard into his groin.

He grunts, releasing me as he buckles. I don't wait before I slam my knee into his face.

"Fuck!" Blood sprays from his nose as he crashes onto the deck.

I scramble to Riley.

I roll her over, bracing for the worst, but there's no blood.

No hole. No wound.

What the—?

Behind me, Theodore growls. Blood drips from his nose. "Wrong move, bitch."

A loud bellow cuts through the air.

Andrea barrels through the door, sprinting full speed.

Theodore turns just in time for her to slam into him, sending him crashing into the railing with a sickening thud.

Her arm rises, blade flashing—and she tries to plunge the knife into his chest. It harmlessly bounces off.

"You son of a *fucking* bitch!" she screams, stabbing again.

"His vest!" I shout. "He's wearing a bulletproof vest!"

Her eyes widen a split second before Theodore flings her off him. She hits the deck hard.

Rage boils over.

I charge and hit him low. We tumble to the floor in a tangle of limbs.

He ends up on top of me again, hands on my throat.

"You lose," he snarls.

I spit in his face.

My hand finds the knife Andrea dropped, and I drive it into his neck.

His eyes bulge.

Blood spurts as he gurgles and claws at the wound.

But it's too late.

"No, motherfucker." I gasp, my voice hoarse. "*You* lose."

CHAPTER
THIRTY-THREE

The next thing I know, officers again surround us, all with tasers drawn this time, and their voices clashing over each other.

"Drop the knife!" one of them shouts.

I let it go. It clatters to the blood-slicked deck.

"Hands up!" another barks, weapon trained on me.

I raise my hands slowly, shaking, my eyes locked on Theodore. He's gasping on the deck, blood pouring from his neck.

"What the fuck did you do?" Briggs yells, rushing to him as officers swarm me. One grabs my arms and yanks them behind my back, cuffing me.

"It's him!" Riley shouts, sitting up slowly and then standing. "He's the one who's been killing people!"

Briggs whips his head toward her. "What?"

Andrea tries to shove past the officer gripping me. "She didn't do anything! You've got the wrong person!"

Pain tears through my injured arm as my bicep screams in protest. I cry out.

"Shit," the officer mutters, pulling back. His glove is soaked in blood. "What the hell?"

I gasp as a wave of nausea rolls over me. "He shot me. And he killed Keith."

Briggs looks like he's been hit by a truck. He nods to an officer, who quickly relieves Theodore of his gun.

"Get medical up here—now!" Briggs screams into his radio, all professionalism gone.

Another officer bursts onto the deck, panting, his shirt half-untucked and sweat-stained.

"Those two attacked me!" he shouts, pointing at Riley and Andrea.

Andrea rolls her eyes. "You're fine."

Briggs lets out a slow, exhausted breath. "What in God's name is going on?"

"Theodore killed all the people on the ship." I try to catch my breath around the pain in my arm. "I have his confession on my phone. It's been recording this whole time."

Briggs nods at the officer holding me, and he reaches into my pocket to retrieve the phone.

I'd started recording before Keith even found me.

I had a bad feeling, but I had no idea it would catch Theodore's confession.

I give Briggs the passcode to my phone, and as he listens, Theodore's breaths become sharp, ragged gasps.

He won't make it much longer.

He won't make it at all.

I stare at Riley as the officer still holds me. I can't believe she's alive, and she walks up without hesitation.

"First, hi," she says with a smile, grabbing the back of my neck and pulling me into a searing kiss.

Her lips crush mine with fire, fury, and fear.

When she finally pulls back, I suck in a breath. "I thought you were fucking dead."

"Officer Spiffy over here let me borrow his vest." Riley hooks her thumb at the half-dressed officer. "I took a page out of Sidney Prescott's book." She cheekily grins as she lifts her shirt to reveal a bulletproof vest.

"I did no such thing, young lady. You cold-cocked me!" He argues and turns to Briggs. "I want them arrested for assault."

Briggs ignores him.

Riley gives the officer an unamused look before turning back to me. "You weren't the only one who had a plan. I knew it was a bad idea for you to walk alone. We had promised we wouldn't split up." She glares at me. "We will be talking about this later."

My hands have been cuffed behind my back through this whole exchange, and I wiggle my arms to try to get some feeling back into them and realize my mistake when my bicep screams at me.

Oh yeah," I say, blinking. "Right. Shot."

Riley's eyes go wide, and she punches my good shoulder. "You ass."

"Ow! What the fuck?"

"You can't leave me. I told you that. And you go and get yourself shot."

Andrea steps up and taps the officer holding me on the shoulder. "Can you please release her? She acted in self-defense."

"Let her go," Briggs adds. "And where the fuck is medical?"

Theodore takes one last heaving breath and then goes still.

And just like that, it's over.

***

The medical team finally arrives after Briggs listens to the recording multiple times and bags it as evidence. They find Keith in the stairwell, and he, as I already knew, was dead.

They rush me to the ship's infirmary. Riley and Andrea refuse to leave my side as they bandage up my wound.

Andrea paces, biting her nails down to nothing. Riley leans in the doorway, muttering under her breath like she's trying to keep herself anchored.

"I need you to fill out this paperwork." The nurse hands me a clipboard.

The words blur on the page. I just blink at it, dumbly and unfocused.

Andrea sighs and snatches it from my hands. "I got it."

I'm sitting on the edge of the cot, and she comes over and wraps me in a warm hug. "I love you," she says.

I smile, but I can't stop thinking about all we lost. "I love you too, Dre."

She squeezes me like she's afraid I'll slip through her arms, then kisses my temple before walking out.

Riley has been quiet for a while, and if she feels anything like I do, I know the adrenaline is wearing off and reality is starting to crash. She rubs her chest where I'm sure there is a bruise from the vest stopping the bullet Theodore fired at her. Her eyes keep darting around the room. She looks like she wants to run, but has nowhere to go.

"Hey," I husk. "Come here."

Riley walks up to me, and I grab her around the waist and pull her in between my legs that are dangling off the cot.

"Thank you," I murmur.

Her brow knits. "For what?"

"You saved my life."

Riley shakes her head slowly. "I almost got us both killed." Her voice cracks, and her head drops to her chest.

Silence stretches between us.

After a moment, I lift my good arm to tilt her head towards me. "That was my fault. I'm sorry."

"We lost everyone." Her eyes fill with tears. "They're all gone, " she whispers.

"I know."

I pull her towards me and wrap my arms around her as she cries into my neck.

Her tears are hot against my cold skin. I hold her tighter, grounding myself in the one thing I can still feel: her.

Epilogue

THREE MONTHS LATER

We spent the rest of the cruise in fog. When we finally docked, the Coast Guard was waiting for us. Immediately, the ship was overrun with uniforms, and they accosted us before we could disembark. They took our statements before they let us leave, asking us to relive every second over and over.

The final death toll was fourteen.

The woman found on the lounger, the two teens, the missing couple presumed dead, James, Keith, and Theodore, another security officer, and then all our loved ones.

The man from the first night really did die of a heart attack. No foul play. Just the start of a string of nightmares.

Officer Smith, who was stabbed, ended up making it in the end, making him one of the lucky ones.

They searched Theodore's cabin and found what we already knew in our bones—photos of us pinned to the walls like trophies.

A journal that cataloged every kill. No manifesto. No twisted ide-
ology.

Just boredom. That's what he wrote.

He did it because he was bored.

We were allowed to go after they took my phone as evidence, and
it's a miracle that we could even function to get to the airport.

We were in a daze the entire way home. I couldn't tell you how we
got there if I tried.

The funerals of our loved ones are all a blur. It was an entire month
of having to relive the nightmare again and again, as we said goodbye
to our friends we couldn't save.

About a month after the last funeral, Riley, Andrea, and I got a
place together.

The media that surrounded us was relentless. Anytime one of us
stepped outside, someone was there wanting a statement.

The headlines that followed haunted us: *"Killer Cruise: How Se-
curity Turned Deadly," "From Vacation to Nightmare: When Those
Supposed to Protect Snap,"* and finally, *"How One Girl Saved an Entire
Ship of People"*.

That one really pissed me off. I couldn't save those closest to me,
much less an entire ship.

However, we found some good information through the media,
such as how Theodore could get away with killing as many as he did.
He was right when he told me he knew where the cameras were and
how to loop footage, but he left out the cameras that he had flagged for
'maintenance' that were conveniently in places where other murders
occurred.

Briggs, as Chief of Security, made a statement that they had
released a firearm from the armory to Theodore and assigned him a
partner per their protocol when it became apparent that things on the

cruise were not normal. The partner they assigned to Theodore went missing before our showdown with him and was later found murdered in George and Hannah's empty cabin.

As we also found out through the news, Keith left behind a note detailing his suspicions about Theodore from when I questioned everything. He alluded to incompetence among security staff and trouble within the hierarchy after finding out that Theodore and Briggs had worked together previously in law enforcement. He mentioned how Briggs refused to 'listen to a 22-year-old girl' when I brought up all my suspicions.

Keith logged incidents after he realized things weren't adding up, and the news alluded to Briggs not wanting to mistrust his old friend Theodore and ignoring the evidence that Keith had prevented.

Keith died a hero trying to stop a psychotic murderer, and the sad truth of it is that no one would listen to him either.

Now that we're back on land, none of us could stand the idea of being alone. Or apart. We know we need therapy eventually, but we're not ready.

Right now, we're just trying to breathe. Trying to remember what it feels like to be safe.

And holding on to each other like it's the only thing keeping us above water.

"Hey, babe!" Riley calls from the front door, a pile of mail in her hands. "You've got a letter."

She greets me with a warm but distant kiss, like her smile has forgotten how to reach her eyes, and hands me a white envelope.

No return address. No markings. Just my name.

My fingers tremble as I open it.

A postcard slips out.

A cruise ship on the front.

I flip it over.

Four words in blocky handwriting:

We'll see you soon.

I freeze, frowning, before shivering and tossing it aside.

"No fucking way am I ever going on another cruise."

I grab Riley by the waist and pull her into me.

"Come on," I say, smiling. "Andrea won't be home for another hour."

We head to the bedroom, but once we reach the doorway, I take one last glance to where I threw the postcard, the feeling it leaves clawing at my mind.

www.ingramcontent.com/pod-product-compliance
Lightning Source LLC
Chambersburg PA
CBHW021030130626
46552CB00005B/1772